Does
Glitter
Count as
Camouflage?

Helen Salter grew up in South London, but didn't really grow up at all, and still firmly believes she will one day live next door to a chocolate factory with Jude Law. Before writing, Helen had a variety of jobs, including selling aerial photographs door-to-door in the Chicago suburbs, teaching English to teenagers in Paris and working as a tour guide for American students in Europe. Helen now likes sitting cross-legged writing on her laptop, pretending she is Carrie Bradshaw from *Sex and the City* (but in East Croydon, not New York).

Does Glitter Count as Camouflage?

Helen Salter

Piccadilly Press • London

Thanks very much to the whole team at Piccadilly for their talent and enthusiasm, especially Anne, Brenda, Melissa and Margot. I am also very grateful to my friends and family who continue to forgive me for always being on the Eurostar and/or voluntarily chained to my laptop. And, finally, thanks to all the readers who got in touch to say they liked Does Snogging Count as Exercise? *– for unknowingly making my day.*

First published in Great Britain in 2007
by Piccadilly Press Ltd,
5 Castle Road, London NW1 8PR
www.piccadillypress.co.uk

Text copyright © Helen Salter, 2007

A catalogue record for this book is available from the British Library

ISBN-13: 978 1 85340 913 4 (trade paperback)

3 5 7 9 10 8 6 4 2

Printed in the UK by CPI Bookmarque, Croydon, CR0 4TD
Typeset by M Rules, London, based on a design by Louise Millar
Cover design by Simon Davies
Set in Melanie BT, Stone and Regular Joe

Papers used by Piccadilly Press are produced from forests grown and
managed as a renewable resource, and which conform to the
requirements of recognised forestry accreditation schemes.

To my mum

Carry On Snogging

'Poppy, I'm ready to go back to school.'

'Are you mad?'

OK, it was only the first day of the summer holidays. But she didn't know what I was going to say next.

'Listen – Luke just kissed me!'

'Oh my God!' Poppy shrieked. I am sure I heard her in stereo, since she only lives just up the road. She repeated, incredulously, 'Luke?'

'Yes, Luke. You know? Your brother? Floppy hair? Picture in the dictionary under "gorgeous"? Just *imagine* telling everyone at school.'

Maybe that was the wrong thing to be considering, but it was a factor, I think. At Burlington Girls', everyone knows who everyone fancies. And everyone knew I fancied Poppy's amazing sixteen-year-old brother Luke. I had done ever since Poppy and I met at the start of secondary school, when we were forced to get the bus together by our parents, who were concerned we were permanently on the verge of getting mugged. (As if we had anything worth stealing – our revolting purple and grey school scarves, perhaps?) Starting Year Ten with Luke as my boyfriend was going to be a major triumph. It had simply never happened to me before – that thing where you come back after the summer holidays and run into school with some showstopping, jaw-dropping news and everyone crowds round you and gets all distracted in assembly. In fact, my life was usually just a long list of things I was *not* doing:

Holly Stockwell Is Not Typically:

1. *Sneaking into wild clubs every night with fake ID.*
2. *Leaping casually into the back of convertibles.*
3. *Wowing the most gorgeous boy in town with an unexpected makeover.*

In short, this was South London, not America.

'Have you, er – gone over it all in your head in case it was actually a dream?' asked Poppy, apparently unconvinced my life finally resembled that of a Proper Teenager in America. 'Were there any weird inconsistencies, you know, like tidal waves, aliens, etc?'

'Oh yes, you're right, it was just a dream,' I said, deadpan. At the ensuing silence, I continued, 'Of course it was real! I was just thinking about packing for our holiday, and Luke whistled up to my window from the street and said he had a spare mobile I could have, because he knew mine was a bit old. Then he climbed up onto the porch below my bedroom window so he could pass it to me! It was so romantic, like *Romeo and Juliet* or something. And then he kissed me!' I paused for breath.

'On the lips?'

'Yes. Slowly!'

'Tongues?'

I paused. 'No. But still! That Year Twelve girl, Lorraine, was

2

walking past on her mobile. So it was a bit public. Otherwise I reckon he might have snogged me properly.'

'Then what?'

'He grinned and jumped down and sort of waved goodbye, then went back to your house.'

'So, did he ask you out or what?' said Poppy.

'No – but I haven't spoken to him about it yet, have I? It was only just now! I'll, you know, bump into him naturally at some point before we go away.'

'Well, we're going tomorrow! I'll ask him about it for you.'

Alarm bells went off in my head at the tactless things Poppy might say – not to mention Luke knowing we'd been talking about it . . .

'No,' I said decidedly, followed by, 'Thanks, though!'

I was glad I'd managed not to tell her she would embarrass me beyond belief.

But when *was* I going to see Luke? After successfully pleading with our parents to allow Poppy and me to go on our first trip away – an organised group camping holiday to Cornwall – I now didn't want to go! It was hugely ironic. Even after we got back home, Poppy's family would be going away again, to stay with Poppy's grandparents!

'The train is at two tomorrow,' said Poppy. 'My mum says we've got to leave here at one. Come over half an hour early or something. You can do some of your natural bumping-into-Luke then.'

OK. Question. If someone said to come over at twelve-thirty, was it rude to go earlier? At like, say, eight a.m.?

I had already been up since seven staring at the time on my new mobile. What if I had a really good excuse for Poppy's mum when she opened the door? You know, 'Poppy did say, "half an hour early *or something*".' Or (less realistic), 'I thought eight a.m. was really near to twelve-thirty? I missed the lesson on telling the time in infants' school.'

But I am the world's worst liar, so I just went downstairs for some orange juice, forgetting Mum would be up. She was in the kitchen, bottle of water in hand, warming up for her morning run. She was flexing her legs in a bright orange tracksuit, which made her look like an energetic satsuma.

'Why are you up so early?' said Mum suspiciously.

Hmm. She is just not one of those mothers to whom you can say, 'Oh, yesterday Luke jumped onto the porch and kissed me. It was like *Romeo and Juliet*. And today between twelve-thirty and one o'clock he will run towards me in slow motion and kiss me again, but this time with tongues.'

In fact, thank God Mum had been out at badminton when Luke came round. When Mum is not doing sport, she is eaves-dropping on me to check I am not secretly going out with a drug dealer or tattooing obscenities on my forehead.

Mum eyed the full travel bag I was carrying, which unfortunately ruled out claims that I was up early to pack.

'I thought there might be a problem getting to Poppy's due to, er . . . adverse weather conditions,' I said, inspired. I gestured out-side to where, unfortunately, a beautiful, balmy summer's day was developing.

Mum just looked blankly at me, which she does quite often. It's

4

one advantage of being deemed completely bizarre by your family – they almost expect not to understand you. While actually I am perfectly normal, Ivy, Jamie, Mum and Dad are all sports mad. They can never figure out why I enjoy hanging out with Poppy, watching tons of films or reading, when I could play rounders with them in colour-coordinated sportswear. I do keep active – I walk a lot and eat healthily too – my family are just extremists. And isn't the Government always saying that extremism is dangerous?

In fact, I should really just go and join Poppy's family. I doubt anyone here would mind. Four is a much better number for team games and I am only the middle child, neither the favourite oldest daughter like Ivy, nor the cute younger child like Jamie. The only problem, of course, would be that Luke would be a brother-type person rather than the Love of My Life. Not ideal.

'Don't forget to pack your cagoule,' said Mum randomly.

'What do you mean?'

Mum showed me a list of things to take that they'd sent her about the Cornwall holiday. She had circled three:

Cagoule
Sturdy boots
Tea towel

It was a bit strange, if you ask me. I had heard what these holidays were like. It must have been so that parents wouldn't think the holiday was too outrageous. They could hardly say, 'Bring a bikini and a bottle of vodka', could they?

'I don't own a cagoule,' I said triumphantly.

'You can borrow mine.'

I wanted to say that you can't really sip cocktails in a cagoule. It lacks the right *je ne sais quoi*. But I didn't. With Mum, I am always a bit on the non-confrontational side.

'What have you got in there?' continued Mum, looking at my bag.

'Clothes. A few books.'

Mum opened her mouth but then, unusually, didn't make any weary comments about me reading too much. Maybe my meticulous coaching (fourteen years of sitting around with a library book) was finally paying off?

'OK, well – here's a tea towel. Did you pack your boots?'

'Yes!'

Mum gave me a Look. 'Your wellington boots, not your brown suede ones.'

Damn.

I went back upstairs and sat around. Should I start walking slowly? You know, in case my bag for camp slowed me down?

The Incredible Journey

'Why didn't he French kiss you?' asked Sasha blearily. It was twelve-twenty-eight and I had just started the epic two-minute walk to Poppy's house.

I had clearly woken Sasha up. The thing is, she already had a boyfriend, Darren, and could therefore prioritise optional things like sleep on Saturday mornings. Sasha had been my friend ever since infants' school, though she had her own gang of outside-school friends and lived quite far away, so over the summer we pretty much just caught up over the phone.

She was spoiling my plan, though. I had phoned her so I would look popular and busy in case it was Luke who opened the door at Poppy's, and now she was asking difficult questions!

'What do you mean, why didn't he French kiss me? Should I have asked him to stick his tongue in my mouth?'

I had to slow down and do little mouse-type steps in order to resolve this before getting to Poppy's door. I was speaking in low tones – partly from the effort of little mouse-type steps combined with my heavy bag – but also from suppressed outrage. Why did everyone keep questioning it? I mean, he wouldn't have done it if he wasn't interested, would he? This was just the start!

'No, but are you sure he wants to go out with you now?' said Sasha.

'It was amazing,' I said, wounded. 'It felt really *promising*. I'm on my way round to talk to him!'

I spotted Lorraine coming out of her house and abruptly went back to walking normally. Instead of blanking me totally, she looked at me! Even people from soon-to-be-Year-Twelve were taking notice of me now I had snogged Luke!

'Maybe let Luke make the first move,' said Sasha hesitantly. 'A kiss is great, but – you know, it wasn't dead passionate or anything. If you act cool you can figure out exactly what's going on. It's less risky and embarrassing that way.'

Not passionate? I know Sasha is really cool and knows about These Things, but she hadn't *been there*. I ended up sacrificing my cool I'm-on-the-phone moment to say, 'I've got to go – I'm outside Poppy's.'

I arranged my features into an alluring, braces-hidden smile and knocked on the door in a state of breathless anticipation, but it was just Poppy's mum who answered. It was almost like a normal visit, which was hilarious because everything was different now!

On the way up to Poppy's room I was hugely tempted to knock on Luke's bedroom door and snog him immediately. But at the end of the day it was Poppy who had invited me round, not Luke, and I didn't want her to think I was abusing my position as Best Friend. Things were only just back to normal after last term, when she had gone off with Claudia, this girl from our Year. It had been totally awful. Apparently dissatisfied with simply stealing my best friend, Claudia had then tried to get together with Luke! I still felt sick at my memories of Claudia parading Luke in front of my nose. Thank God it turned out he wasn't interested. So, I could have warned Poppy at the time that Claudia was a ruthless, attention-seeking boy magnet. But Poppy hadn't realised Claudia's true colours until Claudia had gone off with Jez, Poppy's long-term crush! All this while Claudia was supposed to be matchmaking them! The accepted theory was that, while Claudia masqueraded as a rich, half-Italian fourteen-year-old girl with gorgeous dark hair, underneath she was just a big, spiky monster with a make-up bag where its heart should be.

As I went up Poppy's stairs I recalled the other, more radical theory, the one that kept nice people like my friend Jo speaking to Claudia. This theory was that Claudia was OK really and Jez had simply been there when she was feeling low and needed some attention.

I guess that in a completely factual, itsy-bitsy-detail kind of way, Poppy and Jez weren't *actually* going out when Claudia swiped him from under Poppy's nose. But since when did you have to be completely factual to know what is right and wrong?

Anyway, I found Poppy sitting on her bedroom floor, visibly fizzing with excitement as she piled brightly coloured T-shirts and strappy sandals into a big, pale pink holdall. I looked at her stuff with amusement. Apart from her huge first-aid kit for any medical emergencies, Poppy and I could have just shared one bag – we'd packed pretty much identically.

I triumphantly held up the magazine which I'd carried over

9

separately so it wouldn't get squashed in my bag. (OK, I broke into my holiday money, but it had free flip-flops worth ten pounds! So, really, it was an investment purchase.)

'Ooh, can I borrow those on holiday?' said Poppy.

'Of course.'

Poppy fished Claudia's brochure out of her bag and browsed it reflectively. It was Claudia and Jo's holiday that had inspired ours. Poppy's mum had booked ours through a different company which didn't have its own brochure, and OK, our holiday was only in Cornwall, not Spain, but it was the same sort of deal. Fourteen- to eighteen-year-olds, tons of late night discos and stuff, plus lazing around on the beach during the day! In fact, Jo had told us that Jez wasn't too happy about Claudia going on her holiday, because apparently there were always tons more boys than girls. Brilliant!

'Mum made me pack a cagoule and a tea towel,' I said, giggling.

Poppy laughed. 'We won't need any of that. Just, you know, sun cream.'

'And phone credit for calling Luke.'

'And shades.'

'And – and some of those little parasols that go in your drink, so we look cool in all the photos.'

We looked with anticipation at Claudia's brochure. One page had an image of a nightclub full of tanned teenagers dancing, plus another of a pool with some gorgeous, tanned lifeguards. Opposite was a big group photo taken on a beach at sunset.

Poppy and I were very organised and grown-up and made lists of all the things we wanted to do on holiday:

My List

1. *Have people admire my new free flip-flops.*
2. *Phone Luke a lot and get him to send me a photo of himself so the other girls at camp melt with envy.*

Poppy's List

1. *Meet Gorgeous, Tanned Lifeguard.*
2. *Have Gorgeous, Tanned Lifeguard put his arm around Poppy and get a photo taken.*

Poppy started jiggling up and down with poorly repressed excitement and asked, 'So, do you think it was true, what Poo-brains told us about people going for midnight swims on these holidays?'

I took it that Poo-brains was the latest name for Claudia.

'I don't know. But discos and stuff most nights, definitely. Maybe even every night. Er, Poppy – you're rocking the floor.'

'But – right —' Poppy continued, struggling to control her excitement. 'What do I do if I get together with one of the eighteen-year-olds and he wants to go down to the beach and *do stuff*?'

'Well, how far would you want to go?' I said, a) checking her mum wasn't at the bedroom door, which was slightly open and b) wondering whether to say, 'You have to feel ready and not be pressured', like an agony aunt from *Sugar*. The thing is, I'd had one proper French kiss before now with a random boy called Charlie, but Poppy hadn't even got round to snogging anyone yet! Let alone 'doing stuff'.

'I don't know. What if I like him a lot?'

I hesitated. 'You would . . . I don't know, look at the stars and stuff —'

11

'— and snog —'

'And snog, but not let him do anything major.'

'What counts as major?' said Poppy, adding, 'Come on, imagine it's you.'

I couldn't imagine it. When I closed my eyes, all I got was Luke. Which reminded me I had to go and talk to him soon, before we left. I adjusted the pile of denim and coloured tops in Poppy's holdall so that it stood a chance of closing. As holdalls go, this one wasn't living up to its name.

'With an eighteen-year-old,' prompted Poppy.

'On the beach, in the moonlight . . .' I said, trying hard. 'With my new flip-flops on?'

'If you like. Where do you stop?'

'Um – I don't know.' I guessed, 'Anything involving unzipping my clothes?'

There was a light tap on the door and Luke stuck his head round!

'You OK, ladies?' he said.

Nightmare – how long had he been standing there? He looked sort of surprised, and I wondered whether this was because of the imaginary unzipping or because I hadn't gone to see him yet. Mmm, he looked all lean and arty and delicious. (Floppy dark brown hair, green eyes – yum.)

I opened my mouth but couldn't exactly say, 'It's only Poppy who wants to do that! Not me!' And, well, he sounded bright enough. Maybe he hadn't heard anything. Then I thought of Sasha's doubts. Maybe he had heard but he didn't care?

'Fine!' I replied, hoping the next thing Luke said would give me a clue.

12

But he looked at Poppy's bag on the floor, then just said, 'Well, have a great time! I'll just be here, working. Top-notch TVs don't pay for themselves.'

And with that he turned and went back to his room!

If I hadn't been stricken with doubts, I would have immediately started imagining Luke and me watching our favourite films together in his room on a big, top-of-the-range screen. It is so cool that he loves DVDs and stuff too. But I realised I had no idea at all what Luke was thinking. Did he overhear our stupid conversation? Poppy started it! And I wasn't being serious. Did he think that I was keen to pull someone on holiday? Had he sounded a bit flat simply because he didn't fancy his summer job? Or was he not interested and I had read the whole situation wrongly? It hadn't seemed possible before – everything had seemed really clear – but now I didn't know.

I looked at Poppy, needing guidance, reassurance and, ideally, a bit of chocolate. But she just opened her mouth and went, 'And what if we went for a midnight swim and my top got wet? Would I take it off or would that be too much?'

I didn't think Poppy was going to have to cross that bridge for a while. She hadn't even met anyone yet.

'I'm going to talk to Luke quickly,' I said, standing up. Far better to just go and talk to him than try to read his mind.

I slipped out onto the upstairs landing and towards Luke's room at the front of the house. His door was locked as usual. It bore a barrage of *Keep Out* signs that his best friend Craig had given him. I knew the keep-out signs weren't for me. However my thoughts suddenly flashed back to last week, when Luke was a distant lust object who had barely started speaking to me. Could I genuinely ask him out? Sasha had asked all that stuff about how I was going to act. What was I going to say exactly? 'Don't be jealous of the imaginary eighteen-year-olds?' Possibly a bit pre-sumptuous, when I didn't even know if he wanted anything more to happen. And what if he said, 'Why would I be interested in a fourteen-year-old with fixed braces, tangly light brown hair and a slightly large bottom?' Oh God. Nothing was certain.

Then Poppy's mum called from downstairs, 'Girls, are you ready? Come and put your bags in the car!'

Things suddenly seemed really complicated. So, I turned and went back to Poppy's room.

Holly and Poppy's Excellent Adventure

Poppy and I finally arrived early in the evening at a tiny train station somewhere in Cornwall. We were met by a woman called Liz, wearing a badge labelled *Holiday Leader*.

As Liz led us towards a bashed-up-looking blue minibus, Poppy asked, 'Who else is going to be here?'

'All the gorgeous eighteen-year-old boys who have arrived,' I said under my breath.

'But unfortunately none of the other girls could make it,' Poppy finished, grinning.

'Well, you two are sharing a tent with two girls, Tess and Rachel,' Liz replied, scanning a clipboard. 'And in total there are fifty other boys and girls in the eleven to fifteen age group.'

'Hold on – eleven to fifteen?' Poppy's voice sounded a bit shaky. She nearly dropped her bag.

Oh no oh no oh no, repeated itself, like an alarm bell, inside my head. I hoped that no one else could hear it. Fourteen to eighteen! It was supposed to be fourteen to eighteen!

'Yes, why?' said Liz, as she took the keys to the minibus from the pocket of her sensible woolly fleece.

'No reason,' said Poppy, in a poor attempt to sound unconcerned. She shot me a despairing look. If we had been by ourselves we would have had our heads in our hands.

One minibus journey later, we found ourselves trudging across a field towards a row of wigwams clearly dating back to . . . whenever wigwams were invented. We were on a clifftop so it was pretty windy.

'Eleven to fifteen!' I echoed despondently as soon as Liz was out of range. Had they concealed the age range? Or had we just assumed it would be the same as with Claudia and Jo's company? This was really bad. Worse than when you get offered an After Eight and then find only wrappers left in the box. We were going to spend our entire holiday being annoyed by small children not big enough to sweep us off our feet, even if we wanted them to.

'At least we won't care if we have to wear our cagoules,' Poppy said, clearly trying to look on the bright side.

'I am sure everything else will be the same as Claudia's brochure,' I said. 'You know, the discos and midnight swims and stuff.'

We were interrupted by a call from Liz across the windswept field.

'Bing or eee ows laya!' we heard indistinctly. 'Or ernoo oshup erneye!'

'What?' I asked Poppy. We stared. Liz was miming a square shape with her hands.

16

'Tea towels,' said Poppy slowly. 'We should bring our tea towels later. It's our turn to wash up tonight.'

We turned in grim silence towards our tent. I searched for something positive to say. Finding nothing, I switched to my favourite topic.

'I never got time to call everyone about Luke!' I said, as we unzipped the canvas door and stepped inside the tent. At least if no one was impressed with our washing up-style holiday, they would be impressed by my snogging triumph.

Something in Poppy's reaction wasn't quite right. It might have been the way she suddenly looked really interested in the top of the tent and said innocently, 'Ugh – are there spiders up there?'

The two other occupants of the tent (Tess and Rachel, presumably) were already there. They both opened their mouths to say hello, but I had a bad feeling about something.

'Poppy – did you already tell people?'

'No!' she said quickly. 'No one. Just Bethan, that's all.'

I dropped my bag in horror. 'Bethan!'

Bethan wasn't exactly a friend, more of an Internet-style news-spreading service. This guaranteed that the whole of our Year would now have heard about Luke and me. Including Claudia! I just had this feeling that even though she was with Jez now, she would still react badly. In fact, as I looked at Poppy, I realized that was exactly why she'd done it. Luke liking me had given Poppy some definite ammunition against Claudia. And she hadn't hesitated to use it.

'I didn't tell Claudia directly,' Poppy said, reading my mind.

'Only because you're not speaking to her!'

'Damn right I'm not speaking to her,' said Poppy emphatically, neatly sidestepping the subject.

Tess and Rachel's heads were going to and fro like spectators at a tennis match, gauging our reactions. From the look on their faces, they clearly thought we had really eventful lives, which was quite gratifying. But actually living through the drama was never much fun. And you know what? It hadn't been Poppy's news to share. It had been mine! Mine! My only scandal, ever!

I unpacked and tried unsuccessfully not to sulk.

Our tent got the standard how-far-has-everyone-gone conversation out of the way pretty quickly after that. Tess (fifteen with dyed red hair) was the most experienced. You can always tell because they're the ones who insist on having the conversation.

'That's good! You have Left Him In Suspense!' Tess said approvingly, when I told her about Luke. She was rummaging amongst a vast quantity of sweets and glittery body gel. 'My Survival Kit,' she added, catching me looking.

There was no comment at all from Rachel, who was only twelve and still seemed a bit miffed at having got the dodgy bit of the tent that sloped downwards. A quick glance confirmed that she had name tapes sewn into all her stuff.

I sighed. 'It's not like that. What if he heard me talking about meeting boys on holiday? I chickened out from going to see him in his room. And he's going to Yorkshire to visit his grandparents soon after I get back! I'm calling him this week to check we're OK.'

Tess frowned as she tried on my flip-flops. 'These are too small. No, look – don't, honestly. You need to play it a bit cool. Let him be in control. You already made a move. You went over there, and he knew you were there, and he didn't ask to speak to you. The next move has to be his. Otherwise you look like you're . . . I don't know . . . *infatuated*.'

The thing is, I did need expert help. This was me and Luke, after all – this was important. I wanted to phone him, but everyone else seemed dead against it! For the second time in one day, I didn't know what to do. I wished I had a picture of him on my phone, to communicate to Tess just how gorgeous he was. It would have underlined the importance of the situation.

Poppy and I swore not to tell anyone the somewhat un-glamorous truth about our holiday:

1. *There was only going to be one disco, on the last night, and apparently it was just in the main hut, rather than a proper club.*
2. *There were no fluffy towels or miniature soaps in the bathroom block.*
3. *The only luxury amenity in the tent was one battery-operated light hanging from the central pole, which had spiders clustered around the top.*
4. *The camp was mostly girls, meaning that there were not enough boys to go around. Anyway, the boys all seemed to be hyperactive eleven-year-olds running about with water pistols.*

During the first night briefing, after our tent had reluctantly washed up, we heard there would be a Packed Programme of Fun Outdoor Activities!

'Fun Outdoor Activities?' I asked, alarmed. That was a strange combination of words to put together in one sentence. (Others go really well, e.g.: 'snogging', 'weekend' and 'Luke'.)

'That's right,' said Malcolm firmly. His badge said, *Head Leader*, but really it should have added, *Grumpy, Middle-aged Bloke*. He was clearly the male version of Mrs Mastiff, our nightmarish PE teacher from Burlington Girls'.

'Optional activities?' I asked carefully.

'Well – no. Tomorrow it's horse-riding, then there's quad-biking and swimming.'

Poppy looked at my panic-stricken face and got out Claudia's brochure, but someone behind us laughed dismissively and went, 'Oh, no – it's a bit different here!'

It was Stephen, another of the leaders. He was seventeen and quite muscular, as if he played rugby or something.

He fished something out of his bag. 'This is our brochure.'

Oh my God. It was called 'Activity Camps' and went on about 'fresh air' and 'bracing activities'!

I hissed at Poppy, 'Your mum said there wasn't a brochure!'

Poppy paused, then said, 'Well, my mum found the holiday – but she never said there wasn't a brochure. *Your* mum said that!'

We looked at each other in silence.

'My mum did it on purpose!' I whispered vehemently. 'I know it! She let me think it would be relaxing, like Claudia and Jo's trip!'

Mum knew I hated sport. She hadn't given up at all. She was now *surreptitiously* trying to get me involved! Oh my God, I thought I was escaping an activity-led summer, and I had stepped out of the frying pan and into the fire!

Poppy said oddly, 'Come on, Holly, the activities will be BRILLIANT. I am sure Stephen will take care of us!'

She looked at him and smiled.

I got out my phone and texted rapidly, `No way is 2 old 4 U` (This being no time for spelling or punctuation.)

Poppy gave me a Look then texted back defiantly, `He will do.`

Less than twenty-four hours later, Stephen was forgotten. We spotted an actual good-looking boy! Although he really knew it. (Knew that he was good-looking, I mean. Presumably he also knew he was a boy.) It was deeply exciting. As we sat down in a hut for the horse-riding safety briefing, Tess alerted us to his presence with a succinct, 'Yum!'

We all looked over at him subtly while trying to act like we weren't. The boy was nothing compared to Luke, but it was true – he did have charisma. He looked older than us, at least fifteen, and was wearing all black, somewhat at odds with the hot weather and the sea of bright T-shirts surrounding him. His short, spiky hair was bleached peroxide blond, complemented by a scattering of piercings in one ear. To top it all off, he was wearing shades, even though we were inside.

Mesmerised, we watched him coolly raise his shades away from his eyes and meet our gazes. He scanned Poppy and me in our summer outfits, paused momentarily at Tess's dyed red hair and black vest top and finally headed off towards some boys, probably from his tent.

We all turned back to face the front, letting the disappointment settle in the air.

'Yum,' I heard again. Except this time Poppy and Tess both said it at once.

'Do you want to borrow one of my tops?' I asked Poppy after riding. I had tried really hard to get out of the event (on the grounds that I was still hyperventilating after sports-related family treachery), but Stephen wouldn't let me. I can't understand how everyone stayed so calm. Firstly, it was a gorgeous, hot day – perfect for sitting around reading – and secondly, the horses didn't have brakes or stabilisers or anything! It was clearly very unsafe. This kind of thing reminded me that I HAD to get out of PE at school this September. I just wasn't quite sure how yet, but I'd do it. Somehow.

Anyway, for some reason, Poppy was still wearing the long-sleeved black top she'd just worn riding. She must have been boiling!

But she shot a glance at Tess's back and said quickly to me, 'No, I'm OK in this, thanks. But could I borrow your black choker?'

Oh God! I was being a bit slow. I gave her the choker with a teasing look. Well, at least fancying Good-Looking-But-Knows-It Boy implied she was getting over Jez!

Tess looked round, observed Poppy's outfit, then went back to styling her hair. 'God, my hair is really high-maintenance. But I like it red. It's pretty cool.'

Poppy frowned intently at herself in a mirror, then leaned towards Rachel.

'Can I borrow that black biro?'

Rachel handed it over, clearly sorry it didn't have a name tag on it, and watched in horror as Poppy used it to outline her eyes.

Out-cooling Tess was going to be difficult in a Cornish field with a limited supply of black stuff, but Poppy was clearly determined.

'Are you sure you want to do that?' I said. 'Couldn't you get ink poisoning?'

'Well, unless anyone's got any actual eyeliner?'

We all looked at Tess, who probably did, but she countered with, 'I thought you fancied Stephen?'

'I did,' said Poppy. 'But I don't any more.'

Rachel silently met my gaze and we shared a moment of mild panic. I was almost relieved when Malcolm blew his whistle (kept on a fluorescent orange shoelace round his neck) and announced that today, instead of Rest Time, the group leaders had got a surprise for us.

'Do you think it is an out-of-season Easter Egg hunt?' I suggested to Poppy, as we left the safety of our tent and trooped reluctantly after Malcolm. I felt a sudden pang of fondness for Rest Time, which so far had involved me picking up my phone and looking at it while thinking about calling Luke. But not actually doing it.

'Or . . . an open-air film screening?' Poppy suggested, visibly sweating in her top as she jostled with Tess to walk behind Good-Looking-But-Knows-It Boy. 'Don't you think he looks like that bloke from that film?' she continued in a Very Low Whisper.

'What film?'

'You know, that film. The one with that bloke in.'

23

I gave up.

Suddenly the people in front stopped walking and everyone behind them fell over each other, providing an amazing opportunity for Poppy and Tess to both fall into Good-Looking-But-Knows-It Boy. As everyone righted themselves, rubbing elbows in various degrees of pain and triumph, we saw that Liz, Malcolm and Stephen were standing proudly next to a couple of climbing frames made from logs plus some patches of muddy earth covered with green netting!

'Oh my God,' I said in horror.

'It's an assault course!' confirmed Tess, as Stephen proudly produced a green camouflage stick and drew war-paint-type stripes on himself, grinning maniacally.

'What would you rather,' I muttered to Poppy, 'write your name in sand with your tongue, or do this assault course?'

What Would You Rather is Poppy's game, really, but she lets other people play it if you've thought of a really good one.

Poppy looked at me blankly. 'Do the assault course,' she said slowly. She is really weird sometimes.

'Why don't you go first, Danny?' said Stephen to Good-Looking-But-Knows-It Boy.

Danny! We all looked at each other, triumphant at having found out his name, but Danny glared at Stephen and muttered, 'No way.' Perhaps he was reluctant to snag a piercing on the assault course netting?

'Yum,' Poppy murmured faintly again, presumably at Danny's maverick disrespect for authority.

Surprisingly, instead of telling him off, Stephen just looked around and located his star pupil from horse-riding. 'Poppy – you go.'

But Poppy looked at Danny and went to Stephen, 'No, thanks!'

What? Less than a minute ago she wanted to do it! Had she changed her mind because Danny didn't think it was cool?

Stephen looked momentarily at me, visibly thought better of it and moved on to someone else.

'Look, bushes,' I whispered to Poppy and Tess, seizing my chance. 'Let's hide until it's over!'

'You'll be seen!' said Rachel, as she joined the assault-course queue. She was pious even when eavesdropping.

'Oh, I don't know,' said Tess, pulling a small plastic tub from the pocket of her fleece. 'Does glitter count as camouflage?'

So, while everyone else got all muddy, Tess, Poppy and I sat behind the bush, put glitter on our faces and talked about Danny and Luke!

Live and Let Dye

The next day at breakfast, Tess stopped Danny as he walked past our table and said, 'Do you want to join us, Danny?'

Poppy looked livid. Even though Danny then told us he was sitting with Sam (short, not good-looking boy from his tent) – Tess had shown she knew Danny's name AND had the chance to touch his sleeve! Poppy walked off. Five minutes later I found her in our tent surreptitiously colouring in her nails with a black marker pen she'd stolen from the main building.

Then the next day – Wednesday – things escalated further. We had just been swimming in the freezing cold sea and had a rare moment to relax on the beach. Malcolm hadn't let any of us girls sit out, despite my carefully prepared excuse (risk of limb shrinkage). Yet, Danny had once again refused to join in and instead sat on the beach looking wind-ruffled and pensive.

By that time I had worn my flip-flops for a bit so I offered to lend them to Poppy, and she went, 'No thanks! They're not really – you know.'

'Of course not,' I said, thinking, 'Fine!'

She was now ignoring most of the clothes she'd originally packed in favour of a new uniform: her black, long-sleeved top, denim cut-offs, black choker, biro eyeliner and marker-penned black fingernails. And trainers, because, unlike Tess, she didn't own any black boots.

I started detangling my wet hair with one hand, and edging my phone out of my beach bag with the other to bring up Luke's number. I wanted to talk to him, to make contact somehow – even though I didn't really know what I was going to say. The feeling kept sneaking up on me at weird moments – after dinner as dusk fell across the field, or just after turning off the light.

'Don't do it,' said Tess from her position on a beach towel next to me. 'He should call you.'

'Why?' I said, annoyed that I'd been spotted. 'One of us should speak to the other. And I just want to say hello. If you like someone, and get on, then why —'

'Once you've been hurt a few times,' said Tess ominously, 'you learn.'

But before she could continue, I'd done it. I'd hit 'Call'!

Tess, Poppy and I stared, open-mouthed.

I was scared witless by my own power. Why had the phone let me do that? There should at least be some sort of child-lock – oh, thank God. It went straight through to voicemail. I hung up immediately and exhaled slowly.

'He'll be at work,' said Poppy with relief.

'That will still show as a missed call,' Tess reprimanded. 'And if you absolutely must ignore my advice, we should at least be in the background giggling as if there's a wild party going on.'

With that, my phone rang.

'Luke! It's Luke phoning back!' exclaimed Poppy.

'Quick, quick,' commanded Tess, 'turn the music up!'

Poppy grabbed the mini-speakers on her MP3 player and turned up the volume, while Tess clinked two orange squash beakers together. They didn't really make the right noise, being plastic. It just sounded like I was in a play pen with some noisy toddlers. But Tess cried, 'More champagne, Paul darling!' while Poppy, doubled up with laughter, went, 'Danny, please! Leave Holly's bikini straps alone!'

'Shut up!' I said to Poppy and Tess, before adding meaningfully into the handset, 'Hi Mum.'

Poppy and Tess made 'Oh!' faces. Tess put the beakers down. They both reclined sheepishly on their towels. Privately, I swallowed my disappointment. I had really thought it might be Luke.

'What's all that noise?' said Mum. 'It sounds like a party. And who are Paul and Danny?'

'It's not a party,' I said, wondering why she couldn't just go deaf like most old people. I gave Poppy and Tess a Look – they seemed jubilant at their party-simulation skills. 'And there's no Paul or Danny here; it's just Poppy and our friend Tess messing around.'

There was a silence, then Mum adopted a bright tone and said, 'Anyway, I was just wondering if you had done any good activities? Anything you liked?'

Aha! I knew it. She hardly ever rings my mobile phone (being under the impression it would cost five thousand pounds a minute). This was the call to see if a week in Cornwall was converting me into long-lost daughter 'Sporty Stockwell number two', ready to take on the local sports hall in a banana-yellow tracksuit. All this subterfuge was clearly a more dangerous strain of persistence than her former, more obvious attempts. You never knew what someone that sneaky might do next. Hypnotise me into liking swingball? Spike my orange squash with energy sachets?

'Well, we've just been swimming,' I said, fingering my tangly hair in desperation. The salt and sun had got to it, and I was literally clutching at straw. I was going to have to put some more of my new conditioner on it when we got back to the tent. (I'd bought a really expensive one. Officially it was for camp, but actually it was to avoid Luke tenderly running his hands through my hair and getting his fingers stuck.)

'And . . .' prompted Mum.

'And, um, I did an assault course.'

Poppy snorted, in a distracted sort of way. She was carefully watching Danny as he ran along the beach towards us flicking a big bit of seaweed at his friend Sam.

'Well!' said Mum, sounding cheered. 'That's wonderful, isn't it! All that fresh air! And to think you packed all those books!'

Huh. I know that she purposefully allowed me to think this holiday was going to be relaxing. I was dealing with a seasoned con artist! Well, I wasn't going to fall into any more of her traps. Ever again.

'Oh, and we're swapping your room around with Ivy's. I thought it would be easier while you were away.'

What?

'Oh! That's, er, brilliant!' I began. I was in shock.

'I thought you'd be pleased!'

'No, sorry – I am! That's great! It's just a surprise, that's all!'

I'd been bugging Mum to let me swap rooms with Ivy for ages now, ever since Ivy went off to study sports scinece at uni, leaving the lovely big loft room empty for most of the year, while I was stuck in the tiny boxroom over the porch. As I used to point out when I was feeling brave, even Jamie, who was only eleven, had a normal-sized room! Mum and I had talked about it a few weeks ago. However, I never really thought Mum might take action, because it would involve accepting that Perfect Daughter Ivy had effectively moved out. I had consoled myself with the thought that the boxroom now had huge sentimental value, since Luke kissed me at the window. But who was I trying to kid? Getting out of the boxroom would be amazing! At last, the peace and privacy befitting someone who was fifteen in October! I was just surprised that Mum was sorting it all out while I was away, instead of insisting I pack my own junk.

'Is Ivy OK about it?' I said hesitantly.

'Yes. She'll be out a lot this summer anyway, what with her uni project. She's really into it – she's even measuring our heart rates while we carry the boxes up and down the stairs!'

Ah yes, Ivy's infamous summer assignment. I wasn't totally clear on the topic. Heart rates. Exercise. Something brain-numbing like that. Not only was it PE-related, but she was working on it with Mrs Mastiff! She is Ivy's favourite ex-teacher and does tons of coaching down at the sports hall where Mum plays badminton, and Ivy wants to be a sports coach, too, so it made sense. You just had to ignore the fact that it was voluntary PE with Mrs Mastiff, which was simply wrong on all levels.

'OK, well, thanks! That's really brilliant. I'll see you in a few days.'

After I put down the phone, I told Poppy my bizarrely amazing news.

'Maybe she's allocating a bit more headspace to you, after all?' she suggested.

'Maybe,' I said slowly. Could it be true, that with Ivy at uni I was becoming more important? I doubted it, somehow. I was just a pain who didn't like sport.

'Or she feels guilty about the activity holiday,' suggested Poppy.

That didn't seem very likely either. But maybe I should just relax. After all, I couldn't see how unexpectedly getting the room of my dreams could be a bad thing.

'Either that or she just wants to go through your things!' said Tess.

Oh my God. Tess didn't even know my mum, and yet . . .

'That's it!' I wailed, glaring at my mobile phone as if it was to blame for this treachery. I was so stupid. This was just a legitimate excuse to snoop through all my stuff!

'Calm down, you won't have anything incriminating,' said Tess.

'You don't get it,' I said, in a panic. With my mum, things didn't have to be that bad. Fortunately, I'd thrown away those love letters I'd written to Luke and never sent. But what about those unsuitably-titled teen books I'd got out of the library? And the copy of *Forever* down the side of my bed? And I didn't exactly advertise my copies of *CosmoGIRL!* and *Mizz*, either. Some of the problem pages were quite . . . detailed.

I took a deep breath, telling myself at least I had figured out Mum's motives, when suddenly Danny stumbled past us in pursuit of Sam. He paused to catch his breath and said to Tess, 'Nice hair! Very anti-establishment.'

'Thanks,' said Tess calmly, then turned to us and made a face which, if broken down scientifically in a chemistry experiment, would have comprised:

70% Shock
29% Badly concealed triumph
1% What does anti-establishment mean?

Weirdly, Poppy stayed pretty calm and even did the whole pre-tending-to-be-excited-for-Tess thing, rolling her eyes and saying, 'Ooh!' etc. Tess was, admittedly, more Danny's type. Maybe Poppy was going to go with the flow, after all?

Meanwhile, Danny had obviously got bored, because he stopped chasing Sam, ran back up the sandbank towards us and promptly flicked Poppy with his bit of seaweed!

Poppy sat up and squealed (*50% outrage, 50% delight*), clearly pleased that her biro and marker pen had been doing their jobs. Then Danny did it to Tess too, which meant *she* looked thrilled and Poppy looked annoyed. I was just wondering if I could keep up with all this when Danny flicked me too! This meant I had to look apologetically at Poppy and Tess for being the recipient of an undeserved seaweed flick, which did seem unfair considering that I didn't have a crush on Danny or use any eyeliner whatsoever.

Ugh, though, the bit of seaweed was all horrid and smelly and full of sand, just after I'd untangled my hair! I got up and went down to the sea to rinse it again – not great, but the only way to get the sand out. I dunked my head with almost gymnastic-type manoeuvres in order not to get wet anywhere else – Mum would have been proud! But my hair was tangled again. A thought struck

32

me. My conditioner bottle had said, *For exhausted, tangled hair.* Had I made a mistake? Other bottles in Boots had said things like, *For luscious, glossy locks.* What if my bottle hadn't meant it would fix straw hair? What if it was *giving* me hair like that?

Perplexed by the hair-product labelling industry, I turned to look at Poppy and Tess, only to find that Danny was sitting in my place! Poppy saw me looking and mouthed a surreptitious 'Thank you!' Bathed in the warm glow of having accidentally helped, it took me a second to realise Danny was holding my mobile! Was it ringing? Oh God, it would be Mum, ringing back because she'd discovered an explicit problem page. It wasn't *my* fault people kept asking about teen pregnancy!

'Don't —' I shouted, forced to do slow-motion running because pebbles kept going into my flip-flops and weighing them down.

I was too late. Danny said, 'Hello' into my phone!

Poppy and Tess looked from him to me in alarm. They knew I could be in life-threatening amounts of trouble with Mum!

Then I heard him say, 'Danny' really slowly, as if Mum had asked him his name. I swiped at the phone while Danny held it hilariously out of reach. Eventually he handed it to me, saying 'It's for you!'

I glared at him and sat down on my towel, saying 'Hello?' into the phone.

Danny helpfully commented, 'Holly, you're sitting on me!'

I went to move, glaring at him and his seaweed and the stupid pebbles, when suddenly I heard Luke say, 'Hello?'

Oh GOD.

'Hello!' I said again, sinking back down onto the towel in surprise.

'You're STILL on me,' said Danny pointedly. Poppy and Tess

giggled! I could have killed them. It was NOT funny.

'Who *is* that?' said Luke.

'Nobody,' I said fiercely, turning away and squishing the phone really hard against my ear for soundproofing purposes. Hurrah! Luke had returned my call! This was wonderful.

Unfortunately Danny was now chanting, 'Nobody? *Moi?*' in a playful tone. He picked up the bit of seaweed again.

'Don't!' I said, putting my hand over the phone.

The girls finally realised that stopping Danny would be a legitimate opportunity to grab his arm and both went for it at once. Poppy just about got there first. Amidst all this I managed to stand up and say, 'How are you?'

'I'm fine,' said Luke. It was so lovely to hear his voice. 'Sounds like you're having fun?'

'That's just this bloke, Danny,' I said. I tried to locate my flip-flops which had come off in the general confusion, so I could walk away and get some privacy. I couldn't explain that Danny was just someone who Tess and Poppy fancied – not while he was in earshot. Poppy would kill me! However, Tess grabbed my ankle and hissed, 'Tell him you're going clubbing later and it's brilliant here!'

I put my hand over the phone and said really, really fast to Tess, 'Please-give-me-a-minute.'

'What?' said Tess.

'What?' said Luke.

How had this happened? Everyone was saying 'What?' and we were all confused.

By then Luke had said something else and I'd missed it. I tried to rewind my head to retrieve it, but it didn't work. I finally found my flip-flops and started walking away. Thank God! Now I could clear up who Danny was and say the things Poppy and Tess would disapprove of, i.e.: I missed Luke, and did he want to go out with me or not?

'Shall I speak to Poppy just quickly?' said Luke.

I stopped in my tracks.

'Of course,' I said, miserably, and turned around.

'What do you mean, you've decided to call him back?' said Tess on Friday afternoon.

It was Rest Time. Couldn't she just rest?

'Our conversation was a mess,' I told her for the fifteenth time. 'He'll think I'm going out with Danny or something!'

'I've told you! You're clearly having fun, that's all. You'll see him tomorrow night!'

'But we get back too late.'

'Well, the next day, then. Before he goes to Yorkshire, anyway. The bottom line is he'll be dying to see you!'

'I don't know,' I said doubtfully.

'You already called him once on the beach.'

'But what if I just put him off?'

Tess pursed her lips and said, 'It's up to you.'

Poppy picked up her bag and whispered to me conspiratorially, 'Holly, I've got something I want you to help me with.'

I followed her over to the concrete bathroom block. Oh God, she had kidnapped Danny and I was going to have to think of ways to conceal this from Tess.

Fortunately the bathroom seemed to be free from any traces of hidden, black-clad rebels. Poppy produced a small box.

'Hair dye!' I said. 'Oh my God – you got this in Boots? That's why you were out of money for nail varnish?'

We'd all gone on a group visit to the nearby town in the morning. The leaders had organised a treasure hunt which involved bits of A4 paper and pens and therefore was clearly too much like school, so everyone except Rachel had swiftly given up and gone shopping. We went into Boots so Poppy could stock up on proper eyeliner and dark red lipstick. Then, when Tess and I had taken a swift detour for me to spray on a bit of the Lynx aftershave that Luke wears, Poppy had clearly gone hair-dye shopping!

'*Ebony Evening*,' I read, my eyes widening at her bravery.

She looked at me proudly and confirmed it. 'Black!'

'Danny did flick you with the seaweed too,' I said carefully. What I meant was, do you need to go this far? Isn't this a bit extreme? And what's wrong with the way you look normally?

'I've always wanted to dye my hair,' said Poppy.

Instead of pointing out that she had never once previously mentioned it, I just read the pack. 'Fades gradually after six to eight washes. How exciting.'

The packet had a picture of a black-haired girl on the front and a colour guide on the back. Poppy's hair is dark brown (three ticks for an excellent match). Mine is light brown (no ticks). There was a customer haircare line. I wondered if they got lots of calls from girls with gone-wrong hair, locked sobbing in their bathrooms.

'Will you help do the back of my head?' said Poppy.

About five minutes later I found myself massaging dye into Poppy's curly hair, watching black-tinted water seep into the flimsy plastic gloves. I hoped no splodges were going on my new, lovely-but-expensive turquoise top. (It was all Tess's fault. We were in TopShop and I was just looking at it longingly when Tess came back from the till with her purchases in a lovely pristine bag! Bag Envy tipped me over the edge. So I bought the top, using all of my holiday money. I was keeping the bag somewhere safe so I could casually carry things to school in it.)

'Does it look OK?' asked Poppy, her voice muffled from its proximity to the basin of inky black water.

'Fine,' I said, squeezing the last bit of dye out of the foil sachet. Hmm. I suddenly remembered the book *Anne of Green Gables*. There is a bit where Anne dyes her hair black and it goes horribly wrong. Then again, that was written ages ago when people were forced to buy their hair dye from travelling tinkers and not recognised national pharmaceutical outlets.

'What do you think?' asked Poppy, after her hair had dried. She was twirling and flicking her new *Ebony Evening* curls as I scrubbed at the black line around the basin with loo roll dipped in pink liquid soap.

There is only one acceptable answer to that question if you are a girl who likes having female friends.

'It looks really good,' I said, as Poppy beamed at herself in the ancient mirror. It did look stunning, and the colour was even, but I wasn't sure it was really . . . her. It didn't go very well with her skin tone. More to the point, it was as if she was trying to become a totally different person! Though rationally it was nothing to do with me, somewhere inside I felt a bit rejected. Poppy was clearly trying to break away from the way things were before. But what was wrong with when we were both, well, normal?

37

We went back to show the others and found them outside the tent. Rachel was looking at the reverse of her sleeping bag, distraught.

'You probably squashed it in your sleep,' Tess was telling Rachel, calmly making things worse.

'Dead spider?' I asked Rachel.

'Earwig,' said Tess, looking up and noticing Poppy's hair. Tess glowered momentarily before composing herself. 'That's – pretty major,' she said acidly.

Rachel blinked. 'Oh my God!'

'You've got a black scalp,' commented Tess, 'and splotches around your ears.'

'They will fade,' said Poppy defiantly.

'I'm just going to make a call,' I said, using the tension to grab my chance. My need to speak to Luke was just so strong. I dashed over to another bit of the field and sat down on the grass, far enough from the tents to make it nice and quiet. I took a deep, deep breath, then about five more, then finally hit Luke's number. Just as I thought it would go through to voicemail, he answered!

'Hi!' I said, adding superfluously, 'It's Holly.'

'How are you?' Luke said cautiously.

I dived in before Danny or Tess could appear flicking seaweed or clinking orange squash beakers together.

'Look – sorry about before. I couldn't really talk because people were around. I've been meaning to speak to you all holiday, I – I've been missing you, you know? And maybe we should talk when I get back – you know, about us.'

I trailed off because I realised Luke wasn't replying.

'Is this a bad time?' I asked hopefully, as I heard the click of a door. That would explain it. His mum was in the room and he was finding somewhere else to talk. Maybe everyone's mums were impossible when it came to romance? Poppy's mum seemed really cool, though. She had even known about Poppy liking Jez! (Incredible.)

'Yes, sort of,' said Luke, with a tinge of desperation in his voice. 'Sorry.'

I paused before I could bring myself to speak. The Panic Monster had woken up in my stomach and was currently doing an unwelcome dance. 'No problem!' I managed.

And then he said, oddly, 'I hoped you would have got Poppy to speak to me, or something.'

'What?'

'But I'll see you soon, yeah?'

He said the last bit in a more encouraging tone, so I said, 'OK,' and managed to sound brighter.

And with that, he said, 'Bye,' and hung up.

So what did that mean? He had sounded . . . funny. Was he annoyed that I hadn't let him make the first move, like Tess had said? And what was all that about Poppy speaking to him? Nothing was half as clear as I had imagined. I had no idea what he was thinking.

I went back to the tent, half wondering if I might find Tess and Poppy flinging bits of earwig at each other, with Rachel trying to keep them apart by threatening to ban black make-up. However things seemed relatively calm.

'Did you just phone Luke?' asked Tess.

'Yes,' I said sheepishly, thinking, this is ridiculous. I am nearly fifteen. I must improve my lying skills.

'Holly!' Tess reprimanded. She said seriously, 'You're really on the back foot now.'

I have to say, I wasn't sure if I'd just done the right thing. Luke had sounded odd. Had I been too forward? But I thought it was best to be honest?

The Lost Boys

The Last Night Disco was pretty much like every other party. You know: you look forward to it for ages, spend a disproportionate amount of time getting ready and then there is only ever one good-looking boy and you end up standing in a circle while he dances with the best-looking girl. Except in this case no one even danced. In the main building someone had provided Twister, an ancient CD player and a set of rubbish flashing disco lights. Danny just sat in the corner in a long leather coat, talking to Sam and the others from his tent. There wasn't even any potential for close encounters of the Twister kind because Malcolm took charge of the spinny thing and watched over us all like a hawk.

'I wonder if there will be Spin the Bottle at the end?' said Tess.

No one bothered answering. It was all too clear that nothing would happen with Malcolm around.

'Guess what I found out today?' Tess continued. 'Malcolm's last name is Scumton! What kind of a name is that?'

'What would you rather?' began Poppy as her phone started

ringing. She had obviously been formulating a good one, because she continued talking really quickly, 'Kiss Malcolm . . . or eat an earwig? Hi Mum!'

'I'd kiss Danny,' Tess replied, although this wasn't one of the choices.

Poppy rolled her eyes at Tess's lack of respect for the rules of What Would You Rather and went outside to talk. About thirty seconds later, she headed back at high speed.

'Luke is staying behind!'

My insides leaped at the mention of his name, unlike Rachel who just said, 'Who?'

There was a collective sigh. What kind of weird, boy-free planet was she on?

'Luke, my brother,' said Poppy pointedly, 'will be staying at home with my dad while me and my mum are at my grandparents in Yorkshire for two weeks! I just phoned home and that's what Mum said!'

Rachel looked blank. 'So . . .'

'So, he knows we're coming back! He obviously can't wait to see Holly! Why else would he not come away with us?' Poppy paused to give me a delighted smile.

Oh my God.

'I'm sure he's not staying back for me,' I lied modestly. Brilliant! I felt hugely reassured. All that worrying, and actually things were fine. I worry too much.

'How come he's allowed?' asked Tess.

'He's told them it's his summer job at Tesco's,' said Poppy. 'You know, he'll miss too many shifts if he comes along.'

'I reckon he wants the two of you to have the house to

yourselves!' Tess said, jabbing me in the ribs.

'My dad's staying back,' pointed out Poppy. 'He's got to work.'

Oh my God. I had a reason to go round to the house, as well. Mouse, Poppy's pet, was coming to my house for the two weeks (in his cage I mean, not walking over), but Poppy's mum was also giving me a key to go over to their house every day to water the plants. I did it each year, because Poppy's dad was, apparently, Not Good at Watering. But previously Luke had always gone away too!

I explained this and added, 'I've got the key to Luke's heart!', clasping one hand to my heart in slow-motion *Romeo and Juliet* mode and nearly falling over people playing Twister.

'Datsoromantic,' commented Tess through a mouthful of Lovehearts. She pointed the pack at me. 'Dew wonwun?'

Mine said, *Kiss me.* That had to be a good sign!

Just as well, because no one else was having any luck, romance-wise. There wasn't even a slow dance at the end. The last possible potential moment for holiday-type scandal and Malcolm just turned the lights on! Tess said, 'Oh for God's sake, let's go, I've got Maltesers back in the tent,' and we all just trooped back to our wigwam, falling over each other because Poppy and Tess were both wearing black in a black field.

At midnight we were in our sleeping bags talking by the light of Poppy's pencil torch (more discreet than the main light). It was strapped to the central tent pole with a big, yellow flower hair elastic Poppy had rejected when she decided she fancied Danny.

Suddenly there was a distinct 'oof!' sound outside and the tent shook. This was followed by smothered laughter. It sounded as though someone had tripped on one of the guy ropes.

Poppy clapped her hand over her mouth. 'What was that?' she whispered through her marker-penned fingernails.

We fell silent, fully expecting the shadow of a mass-murderer to loom against the canvas.

Fearlessly, Tess scrambled over Poppy, unzipped the tent and stuck her head out into the cold night air. 'Who's there?' she said loudly. Then she promptly reversed back inside, closely followed by Danny!

'Evening!' said Danny nonchalantly, clambering in through the narrow entrance without waiting for an invitation. He sat down cross-legged on the floor, followed, slightly sheepishly, by Sam.

'We got lost,' Sam said, unconvincingly.

There was not much space with six of us in the tent. I resigned myself to a delay before my nightly thinking-about-Luke time. Rachel looked alarmed and pulled up her sleeping bag. Poppy perked up noticeably, finding herself squashed up next to Danny. Tess looked less pleased, finding herself next to Sam.

We all sat looking at these two male specimens sitting cross-legged in our tent. They were both fully dressed for a moonlit expedition in coats, boots and, in Danny's case, eyeliner.

Danny unzipped the tent flap, leaned outside for an instant, then reappeared with a lit cigarette. I have a theory that smoking simply gives people something to do with their hands when they are feeling awkward. Danny didn't look like he needed any confidence-boosting accessories, though.

'None of the leaders approve of me. It's because I'm so, like, wild,' he said, flicking ash outside the tent.

Poppy and Tess nodded in mute approval. So did Sam.

'Not you,' Danny said firmly. 'You're not wild, Sam. You came with Stephen, for God's sake.'

'The leader?' asked Tess giving Poppy a sardonic look. Poppy ignored her.

'Our parents are neighbours,' explained Sam, who seemed to accept his non-wildness with good grace.

Danny looked at Sam, rolled his eyes and started talking.

I was not quite sure what I thought of Danny. From his conversation, this was what we learned about him:

1. *He's fifteen.*
2. *He dumped his last girlfriend on her birthday.*
3. *He is from a 'really rough' bit of East London.*

'You have to be pretty streetwise to survive,' he told us nonchalantly, as if he walked home every night in a hail of drug-deal-related gunfire. Then, he leaned back onto Poppy's pale pink weekend bag, laughed and said, 'Whose is this?'

'Oh, that's Holly's,' said Poppy swiftly.

What?! I gave her a Look, which she pretended not to see.

The tent was getting smoky. A thought suddenly came into my head. Don't they smoke spiders out of trees in the Amazon? I saw it once in a film. They put glass bowls under trees, light fires next to them and the spiders just fall out – clunk!

Poppy, always on spider alert, saw me looking upwards and followed my gaze. (It's funny how catching that is. All that is required is for one person to look up. Someone else looks up too, and before you know it, you have a room full of people all craning their necks, wondering what they are supposed to be looking at.)

'Tonight was good, then!' said Danny sarcastically, saving me from actually sharing the spider-smoking thought with Poppy.

'We knew Malcolm would make sure it wasn't too much fun!' said Poppy. 'We were saying earlier, if it wasn't for him, there could have been Sp—'

She cut off mid-sentence.

'What was that?' said Danny.

'If it wasn't for Malcolm, there could have been Spin the Bottle,' said Tess bluntly. It was as if when God had been handing out a sense of shame, she had just been at the back eating sweets.

I suddenly felt that desire to disappear into the ground, even though I hadn't done anything! Hmm. I don't know if it was just being in such close proximity to him, but suddenly I fancied Danny! I know, I know. It was random, unprompted and a Bad Idea. But maybe I had sort of been surpressing it since he had flicked me with the seaweed too. It had been pretty romantic. And I only fancied him a teeny bit. Not in a Luke-replacement way – not for an instant. But Danny was stylish, confident and, most impressively, anti-sport. And anyway, it seemed impolite not to fancy him when everyone else did.

Danny stubbed out his cigarette on one of his big black leather boots, shifted position to retrieve my conditioner bottle from the tent floor and said, 'Will this do as a bottle, then?'

'There's not much space to spin it!' said Tess, all giggly. I looked at Poppy to exchange raised-eyebrow-glances, but she was busy clearing a space.

'Make sure the lid's on,' piped up Rachel.

We all sighed.

'I'm just *saying*,' she said. 'You don't want conditioner all over everything, do you?'

Sam dutifully checked the top was screwed on properly and looked around at us. Since the tent was round in shape, we were already sitting in a rough circle.

'OK, someone starts,' said Danny, obviously an expert. 'They spin the . . . er, conditioner. And then they kiss the person that it stops at.'

Tess bent forwards and spun the conditioner. It spun slowly, probably not having been designed for this particular purpose, and stopped at Poppy.

'Same sex, doesn't count,' judged Sam. He passed the bottle to Rachel.

Surprisingly, she spun it without a murmur. We all watched as it spun quickly, then lost pace and slowly ground to a halt in front of Sam. He leaned over and gave Rachel a big kiss! (On the lips, but no tongue.) God, I couldn't wait to see Luke.

'Again!' said Tess, clapping.

Rachel, blushing, passed the conditioner to Danny. He spun it once, not particularly fast. It rotated agonisingly slowly, and then slid to a halt. Right in between Poppy and me.

I looked at Poppy, who looked at me. We both looked at Danny. Danny shrugged his shoulders.

There was an undignified silence, and then I simply cracked under the pressure. I didn't fancy Danny *really* – only in a 'why-not, you're-on-holiday' sort of way. Nothing like the spark I felt with Luke. I looked at Danny, swiftly suppressed ripples of lust and curiosity and said, 'Poppy, that's nearer you.'

Danny leaned towards Poppy, ran his hand through her black

47

hair and calmly gave her a proper kiss, right there. A real, full-on snog! Tongues and everything!

I looked over at the other occupants of the tent. Tess was trying not to look jealous. Rachel's jaw had dropped.

I realised I was feeling a really weird mixture of delight and envy. Mainly delight, because it was Poppy's first kiss and it was very cool that her love life was looking up. Also, now she wouldn't feel inexperienced when I talked about Luke!

Danny finally let Poppy go so she could come up for air, but kept one arm around her waist. Poppy was grinning from ear to ear. Danny stuck a new cigarette in his mouth, lit it with his free hand and took a drag. 'Shall we play on?' he announced dramatically.

Suddenly we heard familiar, irate tones outside the tent: 'What are you children doing in there?'

We all watched as the zip of our tent wiggled and rapidly unzipped upwards, followed by Malcolm sticking his head through the flap, apoplectic with fury. It didn't help when a cloud of Danny's smoke billowed out, visible in the cold night air.

'Is somebody *smoking* in here? You boys – out! It's the middle of the night!'

Before we knew it, we were minus Danny and Sam. Poppy, still grinning delightedly, turned off the torch, so we were plunged into darkness. As I burrowed down into my sleeping bag, I really couldn't wait to see Luke.

Sorry, but by the time we got the train home I was ready for a break from Poppy.

Annoying Things Poppy Did on the Last Day

1. *Spent the whole of the final afternoon snogging Danny in our tent, when everyone needed to pack, which meant I lost one of my free flip-flops in the rush.*

2. *Made me take lots and lots of photos of her and Danny on her phone, with his arm round her and stuff. (She didn't trust Tess to do it without putting her finger over the lens, even though Tess was very philosophical about the whole thing.)*

3. *Made me carry her bag because she'd told Danny the pink one was mine.*

4. *Acted like an expert all the way home on the train, even though I French-kissed someone months ago.*

Then she complained about the holiday and the big lecture we'd received that morning, with Liz droning on about 'being responsible' and 'acting like young adults'. (It was so bizarre. Somehow Liz thought us girls, not Danny, were responsible for the nocturnal visit to our tent. And we got blamed for the smoking!)

I spent the whole journey home nodding occasionally while mentally perfecting my Luke Snogging Plan. Would it be too forward to go round to Luke's as soon as we got back? Like, at midnight? I could go round, dash up to Luke's room and throw myself on him . . .

Wow. This had to be what it was like to be Sasha or Claudia, having the potential of *actually snogging* someone you really liked, rather than just thinking about it on long car journeys or during maths, etc.

Actually snogging! Oh my God. I was scared. What did I need to do with my tongue again?

I tried to remind myself by thinking back on my snog with Charlie earlier in the year, but to be honest it had been so disastrous that it was a bit like trying to revise from a vocab test where you got nought out of ten.

OK, Holly, be calm. I thought it all through and made a plan, analytically:

Learning Plan for Snogging Aptitude

Key Stage 1: *Holly has ability to express simple thoughts and ideas about wanting to snog Luke.*

Key Stage 2: *Holly is able to use her tongue to successfully achieve Actual Snoggage, without:*
a) *Being slobbery in any way*
b) *Entangling Luke in her braces or hair*
c) *Alienating him in some other hideous, as yet unimagined, manner.*

Key Stage 3: *After moment of snogdom, Holly has enough composure to formulate interesting and coherent sentences in the form of a conversation.*

'What's up?' I asked Poppy the next day. I was finally on Poppy's doorstep – and she was being funny with me! Funny weird not funny ha ha. You don't spend that much time with someone without being able to tell when something is wrong. Was she annoyed because Danny was gone and it was her turn to take photos of me and Luke? Grr, grr, grr. If I'd not had Luke to look forward to, I would have had to hit Poppy with my remaining flip-flop. Wasn't she impressed that I had managed to wait until the morning before coming over? I also noticed, with surprise, that she was still wearing my black choker. I thought things would get back to normal now camp was over.

'Nothing's up,' insisted Poppy.

OK. Whatever. I launched into my official reason-for-being-there. 'I just came over to check with your mum that she still wanted me to water the plants next week.'

'She's gone out with Dad.'

'Oh – OK. Well, should I pick up Mouse now?'

'I was just going to come over with him.'

There was a weird pause.

'Can I have my choker back, you know, tomorrow or something?'

'OK,' said Poppy, clearly pained, then backtracked, 'But I might still need it – you know, I'll be meeting up with Danny and stuff.'

'Oh.'

'Well, he's only in East London, so we can meet in the middle of town.'

But surely she wouldn't keep up the whole wearing-black phase?

I suddenly realised I'd just spent more time on her doorstep than in the whole duration of our friendship. I could feel irritation flaring inside me, probably out of having spent far too much time with Poppy in the last week.

'Can I come in, or what?'

'I, er – sorry, it's not really a good time,' Poppy said, suddenly desperate. That was when I heard giggling from the open window above the porch.

Luke's room.

Everyone knows boys don't giggle.

I stepped back and looked up at the window. Then I looked at Poppy.

'I'm sorry,' she said again.

Clueless

'Lorraine?' I said from under my duvet, for about the fifth time (in an increasingly small voice).

Aaarrggghh, aaarrggghh and aaarrggghh again. This was awful. Luke was going out with Lorraine, the girl who lives on our street! We only went away for a week and everything had changed!

'I'm sorry,' repeated Poppy from her position at the end of my bed, looking around and picking at a black fingernail. I don't think my new loft bedroom was quite how she had pictured it, either. Ivy's exercise bike and rowing machine were still plonked in the middle of the room, and Mum had piled up all my books in the far corner. *Forever* was pointedly on the top of the pile, with an issue of *Sugar* underneath it, ominously out of place, but Mum hadn't said anything. This made me feel spied upon but without any opportunity to answer back. I guess it was a small price to pay for moving rooms. Although at that moment I would have lived in Jamie's tree house and eaten muesli for the rest of my life if it meant I could get Luke back.

Poppy had come over to mine along with Mouse in his cage, a plastic bag containing multicoloured mouse food and a book entitled, *Care of Small Pets*. As if any of this could cheer me up. Oh, and from Mum's aghast look at Poppy on the way upstairs to my room, I take it she didn't approve of Poppy's new hair. She already disapproved of Sasha after a minor cheating incident a few years ago, and now Poppy too!

'How could you not bring any chocolate with you?' I said desperately.

Poppy rummaged and said, 'I brought these.'

I looked. They were called Mouse Choc Treats.

'No thanks.'

There was a pause.

'Lorraine, though,' I said weakly. 'What about me?' *Proper boyfriend and girlfriend.* That was what Poppy had said. I felt so stupid and insignificant. Lorraine was about to be in Year Twelve, like Luke, and was all confident and Clearly Experienced. I should have known Luke was out of my league!

Poppy looked pained and sighed.

'I only found out this morning,' she said. 'Luke told me Lorraine was on her way round. I was going to come over and see you.'

It was like triple ouch ice cream with chunks of heartbreak. Wasn't *he* going to tell me? Had Sasha been right and he thought there was nothing to tell? Had the kiss meant nothing? I couldn't believe that I had been at camp, oblivious to this disaster. I should have listened to Sasha and Tess and not been so open, rather than calling him and letting him know that I liked him. I had made myself vulnerable and now I felt utterly humiliated.

'When did it happen?' I said. My voice was coming out all

squished with misery.

'Lorraine bumped into him while he was at work last week,' said Poppy. 'They'd seen each other around and stuff – just not spoken before. She ended up asking him if he wanted to go clubbing!'

Why Lorraine of all people? What did she have that I didn't? Apart from no braces and being two years above me.

'What about me?' I said.

'I don't know,' said Poppy. 'Maybe he was just being friendly, when he kissed you. Or do you think that —'

She stopped abruptly.

'What?'

'Oh God, nothing, really. It's just that – well, you said that he had climbed up your porch to talk —'

'Yes.'

'And then Lorraine walked past and he kissed you.'

'Yes . . .'

Poppy winced. 'So, maybe – with the kiss – maybe he was trying to make Lorraine jealous.'

'Oh,' I said, dimly. No one was just friendly with a kiss. The making-Lorraine-jealous theory made much more sense than the slightly mad idea that he had liked me. I only just restrained myself from eating a Mouse Choc Treat.

'Or maybe not!' said Poppy. 'I don't know.'

I sighed, as a big grey fog of misery came from nowhere and settled damply in my stomach.

I blinked and looked at the *Small Pets* book. It gave a long list of things that mice couldn't eat, like orange peel. How did they know? Did scientists have a poor test mouse somewhere? ('The sherbet seemed fine, doctor. Try the orange peel.' Clunk.)

'Actually,' said Poppy, changing the subject, 'be careful not to shock Mouse – you know, no loud noises or sudden movements or anything. He's been a bit jumpy recently.'

Oh, great. Mouse was going to die if I so much as sneezed around him. Pets always pop their clogs when their owners go on holiday, everybody knows that.

'Lorraine!' I said again and wrinkled my nose up. 'She does her make-up *on the bus*!'

Poppy sighed, in acknowledgement of this obvious sin.

'And she's always flicking her hair as if she's a film star or something.'

'I know,' Poppy said. 'But apparently he's fancied her ever since she moved here.'

Ouch. I managed, 'It's like *Romeo and Juliet*. But in reverse.'

'What?'

'Before, it was so romantic when he climbed up and kissed me. But at your house, just now, I was at the foot of the window. And Romeo was up there with . . . with someone else.'

Poppy appeared confused, but in any case I suddenly couldn't talk any more. Did you know you can stop yourself sneezing by pressing your tongue really hard against the roof of your mouth? It works, honestly. That's what I would have to do around Mouse. It's just a shame there's nothing to hold back tears. Luke *knew* that I cared, and he had ignored it. It was just too humiliating. Why hadn't he told me the truth on the phone? I couldn't even kid myself he had wanted to do it in person instead, because he hadn't. I realised now why he'd hoped I'd have talked to Poppy. He would have got her to let me down gently. Urgh – God, it was awful. What would I say to everyone, like Sasha and Jo? And

Claudia would be thrilled.

Poppy put her hand on my arm, then obviously thought better of it and gave me a big hug.

'Maybe Lorraine's all right when you get to know her,' said Poppy, obviously clutching at teeny, tiny, *microscopic* straws.

'Sure,' I said, snuffling. I didn't feel like liking Lorraine. And how could Poppy be going to Yorkshire for two weeks during such a crisis? And Sasha was in Majorca!

'My life is a nightmare at the moment too,' added Poppy sympathetically.

I looked at the pet book again so I wouldn't say, 'Hmm. Yes. It must be terrible having just had a holiday romance with someone you really fancied and then have to go on *another* holiday.'

Poppy listed her miseries. 'Mum and Dad won't let me stay behind from Yorkshire too because I don't have a summer job, and I won't be able to talk to Danny at *all* during the car journey tomorrow!'

'Why not?' Surely Poppy's parents were used to being unable to remove the phone from Poppy's ear.

'Oh, Danny and I are keeping our relationship a secret. They wouldn't approve.' She added for good measure, 'They don't understand me.'

You know what? She was relishing this! Poppy's parents were fine! I was already sensing the answer to my next question.

'Are you going to keep your hair and nails and stuff how they are, now camp's over?'

'Why not?'

OK. So she really had changed and she was going to be different, for good?

Then Poppy adopted an apologetic tone and said, 'Holly . . . would it be OK if I had your bottle of conditioner? You know, the one we used for Spin the Bottle? It's just that, well, Danny and me only got together on the last night and I don't have any keepsakes. And it brought us together! It was fate!'

Sometimes I feel various emotions: anger, irritation, jealousy, etc. And I have no idea if it's reasonable or not to feel that way. So I gritted my teeth and got the conditioner from the bathroom cupboard. There were many things I could have said if I was a more confrontational person: 'That was expensive! And it wasn't fate, it could just as well have been me!' Plus – 'I can't believe Luke is going out with Lorraine and you are talking about conditioner!'

It's Not a Wonderful Life

Latest Summary of My Existence

1. *I am still supposed to water the plants, even though I now can't bear to go round to Poppy's.*
2. *I am sat in my bedroom with an elderly mouse.*
3. *Luke and Lorraine are probably running in slow motion through the park together.*
4. *Poppy is in Yorkshire with my conditioner.*

I bet Juliet never had this. In fact, I was more like Cinderella, only with a lost flip-flop and no likelihood of a happy ending.

You know, I sometimes think I could be *dying* and no one would care. I lay on my bedroom floor for ages being upset and waiting for someone to come and find me, but no one came into my room. No one! Not even when I added some faint groaning! Finally I got up and stared at the wall. A major design flaw of a loft room is that its inhabitants can't even stare out of the window with the hope that Luke might walk past.

Bored, bored, bored . . . God, you forget during term time that the summer holidays are really dull, unless you have tons of money and friends permanently ready to go out. I read my book, tidied my sock drawer, then counted all the loose change from my tin to see if I had enough for a Slush Puppy (I didn't). This is why they never did *Bridget Jones's Diary* when she was a teenager: it would have been day after day of blank pages with, *Nothing much happened today* written on them. Possibly interspersed with the occasional, *Had Mars Bar*. I made an optimistic list:

Things I Feel Like Arranging:

1. *Going to the cinema to see a 15- or 18-rated film with a boy I fancy. (Boys I fancy: 1. Probability of him saying yes when he has a sixteen-year-old girlfriend and I don't know how to deal with seeing him ever again: 0%*)*

2. *(Less exciting but still freeing me from boredom): Staying over at a friend's and maybe ordering a takeaway if her mum says yes.*

3. *(Bottom-rung ambition): Going window shopping and then to McDonald's.*

* This also negatively affected my changes of the other ideal plans: Going to a Theme Park with Luke and Going into London with Luke.

Then a ray of inspiration struck me. Surely it couldn't just be me having a crap time? I bet everyone else was at home wishing someone would organise something cool!

I called Tess first. She answered amongst a din of music and people cheering, and explained she couldn't talk because she was at a live concert in Hyde Park and Rick (whoever he was) was about to give her a piggyback so she could see the stage.

I looked through my phone for inspiration then called Charlotte (a secondary friend, making it embarrassingly obvious that I had no other friends to hang out with). When she finally answered the phone, Charlotte explained that she had been in the garden where her entire family including some good-looking distant cousins were having a barbecue. Her mum had made raspberry trifle and someone was pouring her a shandy, so could she call me back tomorrow?

Finally, in a crazed moment of friendless panic, I called Susanna Forbes, who is really square and who I don't even like. She sounded baffled and then went, 'I'm in Spain!', which meant I had to hang up really fast because the stupid one-second call would use up all my pay-as-you-go credit.

Why was everyone else having such a good time? Why? And why was Tess so cool? We were almost the same age and no one called Rick had ever given *me* a piggyback so I could see a stage. Probably because the only gig I had ever been to was a choir concert at Mum's primary school. But even Charlotte had a fab family barbecue, with cousins and trifle. She had trifle, and I had nothing! Nothing!

In desperation I went downstairs and talked to Mum, who was no help whatsoever. First, she handed me a postcard, with a funny look on her face. Drat, postcards are about as private as writing your news in chalk along the pavement. It was from Sasha saying that (despite having Darren at home) she had met loads of gorgeous boys in Majorca who all fancied her. It was a classic postcard – that is, it only got interesting at the end when it became almost impossible to read. (Once the writing squiggles up around the address and circles the stamp you are guaranteed debauchery and intrigue.)

I put it in my pocket and swiftly said, 'I'm bored!' to change the subject. I inverted an ice cube tray over a glass of water and whacked it. All the surrounding ice cubes promptly fell out onto the counter. Mum gave me a Look.

'Just because Poppy is away,' said Mum. 'And you don't have anything to keep you busy.'

'No, because I live in the world's most boring town.'

'Yes, London is often described that way.'

'We're only near London.'

'We've got a London postcode!'

Oh, a London postcode. Oh well, in that case, my life should be an endless social whirl. If only people with London postcodes were actually allowed into proper London. And had enough money to spend.

'Just wait until you have a job and have no free time,' continued Mum. 'I've still got marking to do!'

Mum always goes on (inexplicably) about teaching special needs part-time in a primary school being hard work. Anyone can see it is easy being the teacher, because you don't have to learn anything or do any of the homework!

'Think of something productive or healthy to do,' continued Mum in that spectacularly futile way of hers.

I thought hard. All I could think of was the business idea I'd had after my phone call with Tess. The idea is that you sell recordings of an open-air concert, beach or motorway noise. Then people can play them when they get calls, and say casually, 'Oh, I am at a concert', or 'Oh, I am in a red convertible,' etc, etc. Maybe I should try to do Young Enterprise?

I opened my mouth, then Mum said, 'We'll be going to see

Grandma soon!'

I shut my mouth again. Hmm. I love Grandma, of course. It is really nice to have a family member who is not always running around. But two weeks in Bognor Regis? It even had an embarrassing name, for God's sake. And my family still hasn't cottoned on that everyone else goes abroad on holiday.

'And you can come to the country club with me later,' said Mum. She'd just joined a smart country club in Lansdowne, the posh bit of town, in addition to the normal, local sports hall! Well, from the sound of it, it was just a gym with some grounds attached for golf and stuff, but it called itself a country club.

'No thanks.'

'You should think about it. There's a Mother-Daughter Sports Day coming up that Ivy and I will go along to. Oh, and I met your friend's mum there last week!'

'Who?'

'Vanessa Sheringham.'

Oh God. Claudia's mum? Mum sounded really proud. That's because Vanessa Sheringham is in a daytime soap opera, playing the character of a glamorous Italian wife. Which is probably not difficult because she is a glamorous Italian wife in real life too. Well, ex-wife since she divorced Claudia's father.

'Claudia's not my friend,' I said firmly.

'But you were friends with her for a bit?' said Mum, visibly disappointed.

'That was before,' I said darkly.

'Before what?'

'Before we weren't,' I said, remembering I wouldn't want to tell her anything boy-related.

Mum sighed and went, 'OK, well at least you could move the junk covering Ivy's machines.'

My books were not junk! And the machines were, after all, still in my room!

I countered with, 'When are we moving them?'

'Well, your sister really doesn't have the space for an exercise bike and rowing machine now she's in that tiny room. So I thought, well, this way you'll have a great chance to use them!'

I took a big sip of my drink and accidentally swallowed an ice cube. Just as I was thinking 'Ouch, ice-cream headache', the penny dropped. The bike and the rowing machine. Getting me to use them was her real motivation for letting me switch rooms! Clearly since they couldn't come to me, she'd got me to go to them!

'Ivy can just go up there and use them when she needs to,' Mum continued blithely.

Let me get this right. Mum had got me to willingly exchange a private room of my own for a bed in the corner of Ivy's personal gym?

Then Mum delivered the killer remark. 'I hope you've been over to Mrs Taylor's to water the plants.'

To which I said, 'Yes, of course!' to cleverly mask the fact that actually I hadn't yet been at all. God, Mum kept going on about it, unaware of the heartache involved in possibly seeing Luke. I was sure that plants didn't need watering every day. None of them were interesting plants with flowers on. They were just green. Plants didn't stop being green overnight, did they?

Finally Sasha got back from Majorca. I called her on my mobile and she offered to call me back, because she had free minutes, but I gallantly refused. (Why did I do that? Mad.) And she wasn't even able to cheer me up.

'What am I going to do when I see Luke?' I asked.

'OK, there's only one thing for it. You are going to act distant.'

'Distant?'

'You know – cool. Icy!'

'I see.'

'Yes, icy,' repeated Sasha.

Suddenly, Ivy burst into my room. I was so engrossed I hadn't even heard her bounding up the stairs.

I glared. 'I'm. On. The. Phone.'

'Just. Pretend. I'm. Not. Here,' said Ivy, casually sweeping a pile of my library books from the seat of the exercise bike onto the floor and getting a stopwatch out of her tracksuit pocket.

Outrageous! Trouble was, I couldn't move to another room without Mum hearing my conversation, which was higher on the Seriously Bad Scale than Ivy hearing! I pointedly got up and walked to the furthest point from the exercise bike, which practically involved climbing into my wardrobe. I lowered my voice and said, 'Sorry. Ivy's just barged in. So what – I don't even speak to him about what's happened?'

'Definitely not!'

'But it feels like I'm not being . . . open with him.'

Sasha sighed. 'What else do you need to know? Look what he has done to you.' She added for good measure, 'You're a mess!'

Oh, thanks.

She continued. 'You made yourself vulnerable, and now look! He KNEW you liked him, and he's STILL going out with some tarty-looking girl from Year Twelve.'

Ivy was cycling really loudly.

'Ivy, can you stop?' I asked her, cupping the phone with my hand. Inspired, I added, 'Mouse can't take loud noises.'

Unfortunately, Mouse chose that moment to get on his wheel and start circling vigorously. Oh, good, PE in stereo. Ivy raised an eyebrow at Mouse, mouthed 'Really?' and kept going. I glared and climbed further into my wardrobe, at which point I noticed Sasha was still talking.

'I mean, do you really want to be the one who keeps persisting and gets stomped on?'

I sighed, because she was right. In fact, this would never have happened to somebody self-assured like Sasha. She clearly knew things I didn't. Hmm. Maybe I *could* act icy? I probably shouldn't be allowed to carve out relationships unsupervised, any more than Sasha should be allowed to do biology homework without guidance. (The last time I forgot to check it for her, she wrote 'orgasm' instead of 'organism'.) Some people just have different strong points. You know:

Person	Strong Point
Holly	*Can identify any chocolate bar blindfold. (Well, probably. Would like to try, if ever get enough pocket money to buy them all.)*

Sasha	Can identify any boy blindfold. (Also, probably. Also, would like to try.)
Mum	Always knows when Easter is. (This is automatic, Mum-type knowledge, along with whether turquoise things go in a light or dark wash and what day the clocks go back.)

When I got off the phone, Ivy decided to contribute to the discussion.

'I think you should just say what you feel like saying. Whatever it is, putting up a front doesn't usually help,' she declared airily. 'Oh, and I really wish you would make the most of these machines instead of sitting around.'

I glared at her. Ivy is scarily just like Mum, clearly feeling it's her right to eavesdrop on whatever I'm saying. Couldn't she just be a useful older sister? Since when did Ivy know anything about my life? Even Jamie would be more help. And I do make the most of the machines! The handlebars on the bike are ideal for putting necklaces on.

'It's too hot to cycle,' I observed, as Ivy pedalled furiously. 'You're sweating like a pig.'

'Girls don't sweat,' said Ivy primly. 'Men sweat, ladies *glow*.'

She stopped cycling and looked at me with a sort of sympathetic head-tilt as if I should be giving her a sisterly hug – you know, like in *Dirty Dancing* when the older sister suddenly starts being nice.

I didn't. I just said, 'Well, then, you're glowing like a pig.'

With that I went and sat in the back garden and plaited bits of grass. The only other option was watering Poppy's mum's plants, and nothing was going to induce me round there. Not when I might run into Luke. Nothing!

Brief Encounter

Well OK, in the end there was one thing that could induce me round to Poppy's.

It was a week later at about ten a.m. I was just waking up from a dream (Luke wandering the kingdom of South London trying to find the owner of my lost flip-flop, which Lorraine had stolen), when I heard Mouse pedalling. Why was it so loud? Blearily, I opened one eye to see a pair of sturdy, shorts-clad legs cycling frantically on Ivy's exercise bike.

I looked over in puzzlement. That didn't look like Mouse. I put my head back under the duvet and reminded myself not to imagine things. (First that Luke actually liked me, and now giant mice in sporty shorts. What next, dancing marshmallows in double maths?)

Then I heard Ivy say, 'That's great – just ten more seconds.'

I threw back the duvet, blinking in disbelief. Ivy was alongside the bike holding a stopwatch. She said, 'Stop!' and wrote something down on her clipboard.

'Morning Holly!' said Mrs Mastiff. 'Productive as ever, I see?'

It was only when I saw that Mouse was quaking inside his loo roll tube that I believed it was happening. Somehow, Mrs Mastiff was in my house. In my room. On the exercise bike!

'What's going on?' I asked Ivy, weakly.

'Project,' said Ivy succinctly. 'We won't be long.'

I pinched myself and blinked a few times. When I failed to wake up, I realised it was definitely real, and that Ivy had no awareness of the boundaries of normal social conduct. None! So, I got up, pulled on some clothes in the privacy of the bathroom, left the house and went to Poppy's before I thought in too much scary detail about what I was doing.

I knocked on Poppy's door and paused, crippled by terror. Two halves of my brain had a little conversation.

If you hear Luke coming to answer the door, what will you do? asked one half.

You will simply hide behind the nearest tree, said the other half firmly.

But there was total silence, so I let myself in. Phew, the house was empty.

The plants looked a bit brown, but I just picked off the old leaves and gave them loads and loads of water, so hopefully Poppy's mum wouldn't notice. I did the downstairs plants and then headed upstairs with the little watering can, filling it right up from the bathroom tap so I could water the plants on the upstairs landing as well. I was just walking out of the bathroom when I heard the front door open, followed by Luke's voice!

'. . . don't know where I left my charger. Probably in the living room, in my bag.'

Oh God. Mrs Mastiff in my bedroom suddenly seemed like a nice, normal morning.

I heard Lorraine's voice go, 'Well, I'm Nokia too. Just use mine.' She continued, her voice distinct from the hall below, 'Although, why are we going back to my house if we've got this place to ourselves?'

I froze, in the threshold of the bathroom, grappling with an unwelcome kick-in-the-stomach feeling at hearing him with *her*.

Luke laughed and murmured something. I heard a rustling-fabric noise.

Oh Lord and God and all available angels. They were going to get it on, downstairs, while they thought the house was empty. What was I going to do? I had about a second in which I could have – just about – made a loud noise, gone downstairs, made some joking comment ha ha, and got out of there at high speed. Unfortunately by the time I'd thought of it, that second had already passed. I made a mental note to speed up my brain in future.

My choices were now: a) climbing down the front drainpipe of the house, Famous-Five style, or b) listening to their Advanced Snogging downstairs. Unless they actually were just looking for Luke's charger in his bag?

I tiptoed slowly towards the banister. They hadn't come upstairs, had they? Maybe they had gone into the living room. If I was quick, I could sneak out of the front door and run like a runny thing down the street. It was a bit of a long shot, since a) I couldn't run and b) it was the kind of thing you only see in films. (And if films were realistic depictions of teenage life, I would currently be shopping in a huge, trendy American mall in a short skirt, rather than stuck unannounced in my dream man's house with him, his girlfriend and a watering can.) I remembered with a pang that I'd once suggested Dad move the family to America in a vague hope that it would improve my love life, but he had said he wasn't living in a country where there were big tornados and earthquakes. I had said, 'What kind of a reason is that for not moving there?' and he had said, 'What kind of a reason is watching *Mean Girls* six times?' Well, as I had told Poppy, you can't argue with someone that unreasonable.

I peeked over the banister, only to realise that Luke and Lorraine were not in the living room but directly beneath me in the hall, leaning against the stairway panelling. And unless he was looking for his charger in her mouth, they were definitely snogging.

Ouch.

It was definitely with tongues.

Thank God they couldn't see me. I would simply have to hide in Poppy's wardrobe until it was all over! Though, I would *not* be amused if there was no space because of all her new black stuff.

Suddenly, though, I noticed *water* splashing onto the top of Lorraine's head!

Oh God.

I realised that, unfortunately, I was still holding the watering can in one hand, which had tipped over as I had leaned forwards! Lorraine yelped in surprise. I righted it quickly but it was too late. She looked up, untangling herself from Luke. Their heads both shot upwards to see me peering at them.

I wondered how long it took the average human to die of humiliation.

'Holly?' said Luke. 'What are you doing here?'

71

Was he bemused – angry – or what?

'She's mad!' Lorraine shouted, patting her hair in a unnecessarily fussy way, as if I'd shrunk her head or something (now *that* would have been funny.) 'Are you going to let her just chuck water at me?'

I didn't like her calling me 'she'. It felt like she was declaring war. I went downstairs and said, 'I am *here*, you know.' I looked at Luke, who looked away. God, I had always thought I would be hugging him at this point. But clearly I wasn't, because my life was just a big pile of poo. PE teachers, not-very-green plants and poo.

'How was your holiday?' said Luke awkwardly. I couldn't figure out why he was trying to have a normal conversation in these circumstances. Neither could Lorraine, clearly. She was just glaring at both of us and stropping about getting her hair to dry.

Then I got it. Luke was just pretending nothing had ever happened. He wanted to forget our non-encounter, particularly in front of Lorraine. OK, then. What was it Sasha had said? Act distant. And don't talk about the situation. Well, that would be pretty easy, actually. I was hardly going to strike up a chatty conversation about what precisely he'd been thinking when he had kissed me, Holly, weeks earlier. So I just said sharply, 'Don't worry, I'm going,' put down the watering can and quickly left the house, shutting the door on my way. As soon as I was out of sight, I stopped, shaking, and had to hold onto someone's fence. I felt terrible. I never, ever wanted to see Luke again.

I got home on autopilot. Really this was an under-the-duvet-type moment but Ivy and Mrs Mastiff were up in my room, so I headed for the garden. Ivy passed me in the hall, holding two glasses of Lucozade.

72

'Oh for God's sake, it's just my project. I won't be long,' Ivy snapped, seeing my face. 'You'd think you'd be grateful. It did use to be my room, you know!'

I just walked past, the misery in my head practically drowning her out. I sat outside underneath the swingball alone, idly batting it from side to side until it hit me on the head and made me burst into tears.

Little Red Hiding Hood

'Holly!' Sasha rebuked me, when I told her about the watering can and then how I'd reacted. 'Why were you acting icy?'

I don't know why she was tutoring me. I had already explained my strategy. I was going to stay in my room, in my favourite red hooded top until the end of the world or until Luke moved out of their family home, whichever came sooner. Easy.

'Because you said I should,' I said, sulkily, tightening the draw-string around my hood so my face was all squished up into the remaining opening.

'But *why*?'

'Because – because that's what – oh, I don't know,' I whimpered. There are certain things in life you are supposed to be able to take for granted, and with Sasha I was not used to being the stupid one. It felt rubbish.

'You're supposed to ask questions if you don't understand,' said Sasha, as if she was our maths teacher, Mrs Craignish, talking about quadratic equations. 'I meant distant and icy, as in *indifferent*. Don't care-ish. If you get *too* distant and icy, you are showing him that you're angry! Angry shows him you are upset! That is not the point!'

'Oh.' Wow. This was complicated. It was hardly surprising I had got it wrong. It was like A-level Relationships or something.

'Where has showing your feelings with Luke got you so far?' I thought about having told him openly how I felt on the phone at camp. It had only brought me humiliation. But still . . .

'Look,' said Sasha. 'It's not done you any good at all. It's made you look weak.' She took a breath and added, 'Sorry.'

'That's OK,' I said. It came out in my tiniest voice.

'From now on,' said Sasha, 'you need to act like you *don't care*. Be calm and nonchalant. Act like you're not bothered.'

Oh God. But seeing him with Lorraine just hurt so much. 'What, like, have normal conversations? I don't know if I *can*.'

'Think about it. You seriously need to salvage some dignity here. Be strong and CHIN UP!'

Wow, Sasha should be a sergeant major. Or the scarier kind of teacher (although she is much better with boys than it is possible for a teacher to be). I thought about what she'd said, then wrote, *Dignity is Key* on the front of my rough book in pink glitter pen.

Finally, about a billion years later, Poppy got back from Yorkshire. It was a miracle to me that the rest of the world had continued having things like holidays and journeys, when I was undergoing such torment. The only thing I'd done in the last few days was to find out that, if I got my little hand mirror and stuck it at an extreme angle out of the loft window, I could see the street. In case Luke walked past. Not that I actually ever wanted to see him again. Oh, and Evil Liam had told me I looked like E.T. in my hooded top, so I decided to have the hood down for meals and stuff. But apart from that I would stay in it forever.

Anyway, Poppy came straight round. I could hear her halfway up my stairs. I suppose it was nice to have her back, except she was shouting, 'Have you gone loopy?'

Fortunately Poppy paused for breath and saved the rest until she was actually in my room with the door closed. One positive sign was that she didn't have any black eyeliner on, just the black hair. Fantastic – she'd let it drop, at last.

'What happened?' Poppy said. 'Luke said you poured a bucket of water over Lorraine!'

I pulled up my hood again and climbed under my duvet (double layer of anti-world protection). All Poppy said when I explained what actually happened was a muffled, 'Ah.' When Poppy is speechless you know it's a really bad sign.

'Say something, Plop!' I pleaded. *Tell me he loves me really. Give me a reason to ever move again.*

Poppy lifted up a corner of the duvet and squinted at me. 'Oh yes – my mum wants to know why all her plants are now just twigs planted in mud.'

That was it. I was miserable. Miserable, and nothing was going to cheer me up, ever.

The Only Bearable Things About My Life

1. *Mouse is still alive.*
2. *Poppy had a crap time in Yorkshire.*

She said it was all old people and the most exciting thing that happened all fortnight was seeing a hedgehog in the back garden.

The next day Poppy asked innocently if she could drop round to my house before going out, then turned up with black clothes and eyeliner. I had thought all that was over!

'I'm going to Camden with Danny. Can I get ready here? My parents wouldn't approve.'

As Poppy redid her nails, I realised fully that it was definitely a pretence. This stuff was only ever going to come out when she was seeing Danny! It was annoying. I mean, if she wanted to dress in lots of black, fine. But she clearly preferred not to for the majority of the time! I suppose it was reassuring in a way – we were both the same after all. But in that case, why go through with it? It seemed a bit . . . elaborate. And Poppy talked about Danny non-stop. It was as if she had never been away. Apparently she'd had to wait for his calls in the solitary phone box on the village green, because she had forgotten her mobile charger.

'It was like Victorian times,' she said. She continued, without pausing for breath, 'Did I tell you, Danny's got a Rottweiler called St—'

'Storm.'

'Ooh, did I mention it? Yes, Danny says you need one in East London, because it is so —'

'Rough?'

'Yes.'

'Right.'

'Oh, and he is going to Ibiza soon with his cousins. *And*, he told one of his teachers last year that he wasn't "going to take any of her crap". So he reckons he is going to get expelled when he goes back to school.'

Poppy got out her eyeliner and carefully applied it, then frowned critically at her reflection. I wondered if, behind all the layers of denial, she was thinking the same thing as me – that she looked really cool and striking but it just wasn't *her*.

'Really?' I could tell by Poppy's silence that this wasn't a suitable response, so I added, 'Great.'

'He's so cool,' said Poppy, gazing dreamily into the distance. I had to grin at her. OK, she was being an idiot, but I guess it was nice to see her so happy.

Momentarily back down to earth, Poppy said, 'Why don't you come? You know, have a break from this room?'

'Can't really. I am staying in the house until Luke moves out, or the world ends, remember?'

'That's a shame – Danny is bringing some mate of his. And Luke and Lorraine are going to be round at her house all day because her mum is out at work. Do you really want to stay on the same street, imagining them together?'

Urk.

I am not really supposed to go into central London, but I didn't have to lie, not properly, because as we left Mum said faintly, 'Are you going back round to Poppy's?', looking at Poppy with poorly repressed horror. (Typical. All Poppy's fuss about her rebellion and the only person actually disapproving was *my* mum.) So, anyway, all I had to say was yes, and I don't think that one word can really be construed as a fully-fledged lie.

Getting into town felt really liberating. It was great. Poppy and I spent ages doing Lorraine impressions, strutting up and down the train carriage, flicking our hair and staring aggressively into thin air. (It was a billion times more fun disliking Lorraine when there was someone to share it with.) OK, well, Poppy strutted. I did my impressions sitting down, terrified that one of Mum's friends would be on the train, spying on me. We were pretty good, although Poppy won. (She sucked her cheeks in and pretended to put on lip-gloss as she walked.)

Then we met Danny and his friend Matt (disappointingly silent, too young-looking) by Camden tube and proceeded to walk around Camden Market. Danny started talking about which bands were cool and which weren't, while Poppy nodded and said things like, 'They're my favourite!'

I raised an eyebrow at her as we browsed a jewellery stand for bracelets made out of plaited string.

'My new favourite,' said Poppy defiantly.

She went to look at another stall and gestured at some big black boots. 'Danny – look!'

'So cool,' murmured Danny. I wasn't completely sure whether he meant the boots or himself. He started repeating the story Poppy had already told me about how he was going to get expelled, when Poppy came back from the stand clutching a plastic bag!

'Did you get some boots?' I said, incredulous.

'I wore a pair like that to school last year,' said Matt, unexpectedly contributing to the conversation. 'I refused to take them off so I got excluded.'

'School's rubbish, isn't it?' said Poppy casually. 'I'm hardly ever there.'

What?

'I always have to borrow your homework, don't I, Holly?'

What?

'And I suppose you've always done it?' said Danny to me, as we left the market and headed for the shops instead. He didn't say it in a mean way, but it allowed Danny and Poppy to exchange a little mutual smile. I was obliged to suppress a miniature shriek of rage. Yes, I did my homework, but so did Poppy! It was Sasha who always borrowed mine, and she was just not that fussed about school! Which was much more praiseworthy and authentic than *pretending* not to be!

After about ten shops all selling identical skateboards and black T-shirts with skulls on, I had stopped fuming. Poppy and I went into The Body Shop while Danny and Matt went down the road for some cigarettes. I waited outside in the sunshine while Poppy was buying a soap. Poppy emerged from The Body Shop and I saw her quickly chuck the receipt and The Body Shop bag into the nearest bin!

'What are you doing?' I said, puzzled.

Poppy didn't respond. As the boys sauntered back across the road, she uncurled her hand to reveal the soap and said to Danny, 'Look what I got!'

Danny winked extravagantly and said, 'Nice one,' before putting his arm around her and setting off. I just walked behind them, quietly thinking, 'What?'

'So now you're pretending to steal stuff?' I asked Poppy, once my slow-motion mind had caught up. We were back in my bedroom, having dashed upstairs so Mum wouldn't see Poppy's bag with her boots in and guess we'd been in London.

'Well, Danny thought it was cool, didn't he?' said Poppy.

You know, I used to think I was clever. But this summer was telling me how little I knew, behaviour-wise.

'I did have to throw away a perfectly good bag,' added Poppy, crestfallen.

I didn't know what to say.

'Don't look at me like I'm mad,' she said.

'I guess it's just one of those teenage rites of passage, isn't it, pretending to steal stuff?'

'Shut up.'

'You shut up!'

Poppy huffed a bit and got out her new boots. They did smell good, of leather.

'Will they make your feet hot?' I said.

'No. Look, what's the problem?'

Hmm. Poppy wasn't usually this defensive.

'Are they . . . really you?'

'I bought them, didn't I?' Poppy said, facetiously.

'You only bought them to wear around Danny,' I said bravely.

'No I didn't,' replied Poppy defiantly. 'I'm going to wear them now!'

She put them on and laced them up, huffing and puffing, then stomped up and down on my wooden floor, which led to Mum yelling, 'Holly!' The boots were clearly really uncomfortable, from the tortured way Poppy was walking. But she just went, 'See? Fine!'

After she left, I got my little mirror and angled it out of the loft window. Halfway down the road, I saw Poppy stop and take off the boots, holding onto somebody's hedge for support, then fan her feet in the heat!

Poppy clearly needed help. I had a quick look online for advice websites. It was useless, though. They only had help for teenagers who actually stole stuff – nothing for people who pretended to.

Summer Holiday

I didn't see Luke again for ages, which was good because I got bored with my hooded top and eventually decided to just be sad in my normal clothes. Now and again Poppy would forget and say things like, 'I heard Lorraine say it's cool that their names start and end with the same letter! *L* and *E*!' followed by, 'Oops, sorry.' I would get despondent because my name didn't start and end with *L* and *E*, but then Sasha would call and remind me about acting Casual and Nonchalant, just like I would remind her to revise before exams.

At least the family holiday to see Grandma was a welcome distraction from my main worries (Luke proposing to Lorraine, Poppy getting done for imaginary shoplifting).

I had a question, though. Seeing as I was almost fifteen, surely more interesting stuff should be happening to me on family holidays?

What Should Be Happening To Almost-Fifteen-Year-Olds on Family Holidays

1. *Getting chatted up by unexpectedly gorgeous teenage neighbour.*
2. *Watching tanned local boys surfing.*

3. *Helping a famous person to retreat from the paparazzi, who is eternally grateful and writes a song about you.*

What Actually Happened on My Family Holiday

1. *Spent two weeks being cajoled into playing games of mini golf, beach volleyball, etc.*
2. *Propped up Coke cans on the beach with pebbles and competed with Jamie to hit them.*
3. *Sat in car looking for parking spaces near jet-ski centres, feeling car sick.*

I drew the line at jet-skiing and wrote my postcards instead. (I found some mercifully vague cards that just said 'Sussex Downs', instead of naff, embarrassingly named Bognor Regis.)

Auntie Jess, Uncle Grant and my eighteen-year-old cousin Will came to Grandma's for lunch one day. I don't know why, but something about being at Grandma's, surrounded by the whole family, made me feel about ten again – incredibly distant from all my stupid hopes about Luke. It was as if this summer nothing had progressed at all and I was still a small child. For a minute I considered climbing onto the kitchen table and announcing, 'I want a happy ending! You know, I walk away from Luke, inexplicably stand still waiting for him, then he chases after me and he snogs me passionately! That kind of thing!' But instead I just asked Will, 'How's the music going?'

Will is a Cool Cousin. He makes music on his computer and once played at an under-Eighteens' night in Southampton.

'I'm pretty big on the Internet. Lots of fans in Norway,' he said, balancing two Willow Pattern place mats in an upside-down 'V' shape which promptly collapsed.

That was no use, as I didn't know any Norwegians. (Astrid from school was born in Sweden, but I didn't think that counted.) Will gave me one of the demo CDs he'd had made. It was fairly impressive, if you ignored the fact that the cover had been photocopied.

This was What Should Happen Now, if there was any justice in this world:

1. *Will would immediately become famous.*
2. *I would get him to play a sell-out gig at my school.*
3. *I would win eternal popularity.*
4. *Luke would turn up and wrap his arms around me in a passionate embrace, etc, etc.*

Instead, Grandma said, 'Holly, could you get the biscuits out of the cupboard, please?'

Fine, fine, fine. I looked in the cupboard and reached past packets of out-of-date instant soup to get the biscuit tin, an ancient Royal Wedding commemoration tin with Charles and Diana's faces on the side. Was I never going to have an interesting life? Was my fate to fetch biscuits FOREVER?

Oh my God! Just when I thought my life was really boring, two interesting things happened! Firstly, my family and I agreed on something, which I don't think has ever happened before. After the others had left we played Will's CD on Grandma's portable CD player, and we had to turn it off! It felt surprisingly nice – a rare moment of unity. We were halfway through a track called 'Maniac

Horrorcaust'. As Dad said, it sounded like someone banging on a dustbin lid while a wildebeest slowly died in the background. Grandma thought it was great, but that is because she has been deaf for the last twenty years.

But secondly, right at the end of the holiday, I was walking along Grandma's street and some boys wolf-whistled as they cycled past on bikes! Then they yelled, 'Nice arse.' It was really flattering! It was just unfortunate that they were only about ten.

I dashed back to Grandma's where my phone was charging, but, halfway through my text to Poppy, things took a dramatic turn for the worse. The phone went *beep beep BEEP* really loudly and then turned itself off! I felt a sense of helpless panic, even worse than whenever I have a netball in my hand. Oh God, what if Mum had secretly installed some sort of anti-adult content block on my phone? It had happened just as I spelled out the word 'arse'!

Eventually I realised it just hadn't been charging properly and that the battery must have gone dead. (Possibly something to do with the broken wires sticking out of the charger.)

In desperation, I gave the charger to Dad, as he is good at mending tennis racquets and punctured footballs. However, after prising it apart, he looked unnervingly confused.

'I thought it was a plug,' he explained.

Great. So now I just had lots of *bits* of charger. Drat, drat, drat. Managed to disguise my distress while saying goodbye and thank you to Grandma, but then I had to sit in the car home for about nine billion hours, totally out of contact with the world! Now and again Mum would talk to us all about the country club, oblivious to what was going on inside my head:

What Was Going on Inside My Head

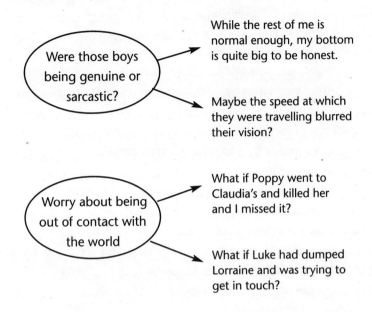

Were those boys being genuine or sarcastic?

While the rest of me is normal enough, my bottom is quite big to be honest.

Maybe the speed at which they were travelling blurred their vision?

Worry about being out of contact with the world

What if Poppy went to Claudia's and killed her and I missed it?

What if Luke had dumped Lorraine and was trying to get in touch?

Got back and called Poppy from – urk – the house phone. I couldn't bear it. Mine had to be the last family in England to have a landline with no useful features like a cordless headset or an extension cord. If you wanted to make a call, you had to sit in the downstairs hall where everyone could hear you. Which was probably the reason why Mum had never upgraded it.

I fired off the key questions first, while Mum was outside unpacking the car.

'Have Luke and Lorraine split up?' I asked Poppy.

'Er – no. Sorry. He's round at hers right now —'

'Have you killed Claudia?'

'No, but only because I haven't seen —'

'Are you still with Danny?'

'Ooh, he's so cool, right —'

'Right, then we're up to date!'

I hung up as Mum walked in, and sat innocently as if I'd just been resting by the phone. Mission accomplished! Mum looked at me suspiciously.

Perhaps unfortunately, Poppy called straight back.

'Are you bored? Do you want to come round?'

'Give me five minutes.'

'Already?' said Mum, who huffed a lot and said that, to Poppy and me, holidays were just an inconvenient break between sleep-overs. (A remarkably accurate description, I thought.) But it's not really her fault, Mum just doesn't understand anything some-times. Like when I left the house. She said, 'Holly Stockwell, why are you forever carrying round that plastic bag with nothing in it?'

'It's my TopShop bag!'

'So?'

So? So? Imagine if while I was out Dad accidentally used it to put the rubbish in! What would be the point of having spent all that money on the top?

Poppy emerged as I approached her house. She appeared to be triumphantly waving an empty tin of pineapple chunks.

'I've got it!'

'Are you sure you haven't lost it?'

Poppy gave me a Look. 'I mean,' she said acidly, 'your mobile's broken, right? Let's do that tin can phone thing! For a laugh!'

'What, where you link them together with string? That's for kids!'

God, it was like *Blue Peter*, but worse. Once school started on

Monday, I would be in Year Ten, far too grown up for such things.

'It's what people did before mobiles!'

'No it's not!'

'Listen, are you bored or what?'

'Yes.'

'So, it will be a laugh. Come on!'

She got a baked beans can too, and we sat making the phone things in Poppy's front garden. Admittedly it was quite good fun. In preparation for Year-Ten-type maturity I held out at least five minutes before telling Poppy my key bit of news.

'Guess what?' I said modestly. 'In Bognor Regis some boys went past and wolf-whistled at me and said I had a nice arse!'

'How old were they?'

'About sixteen,' I lied, calling upon the Law of Exaggeration:

Law of Exaggeration: *Acceptable stretching-of-truth to be used for describing situations such as the age of wolf-whistlers, length and success of your first snog, etc.*

This is as opposed to the Law of Understatement:

Law of Understatement: *Common way of minimising how sad you were as a child by claiming you were at least three years younger than you actually were. E.g.: You say you once wet yourself through laughing too much when you were five, when actually you were eight.*

I expected Poppy to ask more about the arse comment (attractiveness of passing boys, sincerity of tone, possible blurred vision due to speed of bikes), but instead she suddenly said, 'Oh, I got you a photo of Luke! I'll send it to you when your mobile's fixed.'

She showed it to me on her phone.

'This is a photo of Luke and Lorraine!'

'I know – sorry about that. But Luke is in it.' She added helpfully, 'I thought you could just obstruct Lorraine's half of the photo with your thumb.'

Well, it was a nice thought.

'How's Danny?' I said, determined to enjoy Poppy's romantic success, since happiness was forever denied to me.

'He's called me five times today!'

'Wow – isn't that, like, a lot?'

'Oh, I haven't answered.'

'Won't he just be trying to get through?'

'It's just a game! He thinks I'm really popular! It keeps him keen.'

'Was that one of Tess's tips?'

'Yes,' Poppy admitted.

Well, it seemed to be working. God, earlier this year I thought a relationship would be really simple. But they were clearly very complicated.

I noticed Poppy's nail polish had chipped off but not been redone. And she hadn't bothered putting on any eyeliner this weekend. She caught me looking.

'I'm redoing my nails later,' she said, a bit sharply.

I said nothing and we tried to make the hole in the base of each can with the pointy end of a hairgrip, but that didn't work so we used Poppy's compass. At one point I got baked beans round my

90

ear because we hadn't rinsed the second tin out properly, but finally we tied the cans together with a really long bit of string from her dad's shed. Poppy got me to sit in the front garden with one of the tins, while she went upstairs with the other one to test it.

Unfortunately, I think Poppy misjudged the length of string required, because suddenly my bit of string tugged itself free from my tin can and shot down the path into the house. Even more unfortunately, Luke and Lorraine chose that precise moment to walk up the road. They were confronted with the sight of me sitting in the front garden yelling 'Hello? Plop?' into an empty baked beans can.

OK. Calm. Nonchalant. I wasn't quite sure how best to accomplish this while holding an empty tin of baked beans. Even without the beans, I wasn't sure if I could act normal. However it was necessary, wasn't it?

'Hello,' said Luke. Lorraine said nothing as usual. She had clearly been practising her stroppy, silent look, though, because it got better every time I saw her.

'Hi Luke,' I managed, then summoned up all my strength and added, 'So, have you bought your TV yet?'

Luke looked surprised, then said, 'Almost. I'm still saving.'

You know, it wasn't that bad! It felt like a layer of protection, pretending I was completely fine about things. If I didn't seem to care, then I couldn't seem to be hurt and humiliated either, could I?

Luke looked at the tin can. 'Me and Poppy used to make those,' he volunteered. 'Mind you, I was about five. And you've lost half of it.'

Luckily, from inside came the sound of Poppy going, 'Oops!' really loudly, which saved me from a) having to explain, and b) having to ask if he had actually been eight.

'Are you looking forward to starting A-levels on Monday?' I said, thinking, 'Oh good question, Holly. All I need now is to buy him socks and batteries for Christmas and the transformation into elderly relative will be complete.'

'Yes, art, maths and film studies,' said Luke, getting enthusiastic. 'The art course has got a lot of photography in it, so I'm really — '

Lorraine interrupted. 'Luke – are you getting me an ice lolly then or what? I'm boiling!'

So Luke went inside to get ice lollies (he didn't offer me one, charming). Lorraine just stared into the distance without talking, while I sat defiantly on the grass with my friend the tin can, thinking about how, apart from the maths, Luke's A-levels were an impeccable selection.

Then I came to my senses, got up and followed the string upstairs to locate Poppy.

I was so proud I had done it – shown a neutral veneer! I tried to shake off the feeling that I was splitting in two. In all the stuff I had to learn about relationships, I had never realised before that pretending was such an important part.

Mean Girls

The first day of Year Ten at Burlington Girls' really wasn't the moment of triumph I had envisaged at the start of the summer:

Ideal

Getting on the bus with Luke entwined in his arms.

Showing people lots of Luke-with-arm-round-me photos.

Actual

Getting on the bus with Jamie for his first day at the boys' secondary school, entwined in his football kit and science overall.

Hiding my photo of Luke with his actual girlfriend in Year Twelve. (I bought a new charger, so my phone was OK again. Hurrah.)

But I wasn't going to allow things to get me down. Over the summer, you see, stupid things can build up to a possibly unhealthy level simply because you have nothing else to distract you. Year Ten would be a shiny, new beginning: new pens, new rough book, new

Holly. I had already made some excellent resolutions!

1. *Be nice to Jamie, who looked all sweet and vulnerable in his too-big uniform.*
2. *Calmly excel at the first year of GCSEs and be able to take them all early.*
3. *Exude lots and lots of Casual Nonchalance if I ever see Luke.*
4. *Not get annoyed by Lorraine or Claudia, but accept that they are just happy and cool and pretty and I am not.*

At least, that is what I had planned, until about five minutes after arriving, when Poppy and I passed Claudia and Jo in front of the sports noticeboard. Jo had caught the sun over the summer, which made her freckles stand out against her pale skin and curly auburn hair. Claudia was looking dark haired and unmissable as usual in that I'm-half-Italian way of hers (although personally I thought she had overdone it on the eyeshadow). I prepared to avoid them and chat to Jo later, but Claudia saw me coming and said delightedly, 'Holly! Guess what?'

She was breaking the code! She knew Poppy and I weren't speaking to her!

I hoped she was going to say that her mum was whisking her off to a finishing school in the Swiss Alps. But she looked too amused.

'Holly, you're on the cross-country team this term.'

'What?' I dashed over to the noticeboard, thinking she must be lying. But it was true.

The cross-country team.

Me! Despite having spent my life clearly and methodically

demonstrating an allergy to unnecessary physical exercise! I couldn't, I just couldn't run. Neither could I face having to run around Cameron Park in my elasticated purple and grey PE shorts. And Jo was on the list, despite hating PE too! We exchanged looks of commiseration.

'Why?' I said plaintively, as Claudia tried unsuccessfully not to smirk. I was aiming the question at the universe in general, but Mrs Mastiff was walking past and responded, 'Everybody is on some sort of sports team this term.'

'What about netball instead?' I asked her hopefully. If it came to it, I could stand still and swivel occasionally.

'Netball is full. Most people signed up for a team last year.'

If I'd known before the autumn, I could have switched schools!

'Running isn't a team game,' observed Mrs Mastiff as she walked off. 'Fewer people to disappoint.'

Good point.

By now, Poppy was looking thunderously at Claudia and swinging her new army surplus schoolbag in a slightly deranged manner.

'Anyway,' said Jo valiantly. 'How was your summer? Poppy, your hair looks great!'

Thank God for Jo. If she and I could talk normally for a few minutes, maybe we could pretend everything was OK. (Why was Jo friends with Claudia? Why? OK, they both lived in Landsdowne, the posh bit of town, and Jo's parents drove them to school together, but that was about it.)

We said the usual stuff about how great our summers were (you can never admit you got bored, even if you spent the entire summer going to the shops for your Mum), but quickly we were back on dangerous territory.

'Did I say, I met someone?' said Poppy, turning towards Jo. 'He's called Danny! He's fifteen, right, lives in East London and . . .'

When Poppy finally stopped to draw breath, Claudia said to Poppy, 'That's great – he sounds really cool!'

Icy pause.

'That's because he is,' managed Poppy shortly, not looking her in the eye. 'He likes really cool music and stuff.'

'My dad got Jez and me tickets for Party in the Park,' attempted Claudia.

So, they were still together then. I had wondered whether they would survive Claudia's holiday in Spain.

'Danny and I were going to go to that but he said it was lame.'

You could practically see Claudia's mood turn, from conciliatory to angry. 'So – did Danny get you to dye your hair?'

Poppy frowned darkly. 'No! I chose to.'

Claudia paused for a split second. 'So, it was your idea to copy me?'

Poppy glowered. I hadn't thought of it before, but actually they did now look more alike. Except black hair suited Claudia's complexion. Poppy was more of an English rose, so the black was a bit harsh against her skin.

'Mind you,' said Claudia, looking critically at Poppy's hair. 'It's difficult to imitate dark hair. It's hard to get the natural gloss.'

Poppy reddened with anger. Technically, Claudia was right. But I still had to restrain a sudden urge to get my banana out of my packed lunch and mash it into Claudia's head.

Sasha passed us in the corridor, made a face behind Claudia's

96

back and wisely kept moving. Sasha and Claudia Don't Get On. Sometimes I think they are too similar – both cool and successful with boys. (At which point I remember that, unlike Claudia, Sasha is also a human being.)

Jo changed the subject again. 'So, Holly – how are you and Luke?'

Oh, *God.* She said it so sweetly, as if she was really excited for me. I'd forgotten I'd not been able to face telling anyone from school. I should have let Bethan spread the news.

I swallowed hard and said, 'He's going out with Lorraine from Year Twelve.'

Jo's face dropped. But as expected, I'd made Claudia's day. You could practically see her internal point-scoring mechanism adjusting back to the setting 'All Well with the World, Rightful Balance Restored'.

'Ah well,' she said, pseudo-sympathetically.

It was only the bell ringing that saved her from my banana.

I was wrong. Jamie is not sweet and vulnerable. On Thursday he spent an hour on the landline after school, just when I was out of credit but really needed to speak to Poppy about how to get out of cross-country! (Predictably, Mum was delighted to hear about it and only just fell short of implying that my actual GCSE options were a waste of potential running time.) No one ever rings for Jamie! It was really inconsiderate of him. All he said was, 'Yeah man', as he nodded his head. (I don't think he has got the hang of phone conversations yet and realised that no

97

one can see him.) I was trying to restrain my impatience and imagine that maybe he was discussing something of international importance when suddenly he said, 'So you press "Fire" and "Up", leap off da balcony and it take you straight to Level Five?'

What was with the weird accent? When he got off the phone I felt a moral obligation to comment.

'I need the phone,' I said. 'And why are you talking like that?'

'I can talk how I like, innit?' mumbled Jamie. 'Asif and Imran are *cool*. You *know* so.'

Oh – OK. New friends at secondary school?

'You sound like an idiot,' I suggested helpfully.

'*You're* an idiot!'

'Good comeback. Very clever.'

'Mum lets *me* use da phone. It's *you* she don't like.'

'Mum teaches special needs, so she's used to you.'

'Asif and Imran know I'm cool,' he said with an air of finality. 'They are *da man*!' Jamie made a sucking noise through his teeth, apparently unconcerned that he'd suddenly turned into somebody else.

'What about Evil L – what about Liam?' I said.

'Liam's not cool,' Jamie said, running upstairs to his room. 'Oh, and I'm not getting the bus with you any more! Got to look after my image!'

Had I just been dumped by my own little brother for not being cool enough?

'Why's he being so weird?' I asked Mum. As usual, she was eavesdropping quite openly from the upstairs landing. I was struggling with the unprecedented thought that I might be missing Evil Liam.

'Adolescence,' said Mum.

'But I am fine,' I said.

She just made a weird noise.

I was mad. Mad! Why did I ever want to be back? My lists on the subject of school-awfulness took up a whole page of my rough book:

OK, Not Too Bad Things About School

1. *Everybody looked dead impressed by my TopShop bag.*
2. *Sasha drew gold stars in glitter pen on my rough book for being so Calm and Nonchalant around Luke.*
3. *Everyone in Year Ten keeps coming up to me and being sympathetic because they've now heard about Luke and Lorraine. They are not letting me sit near windows and stuff in case I jump out, which is sweet.*
4. *Luke might be thrilled by the amazing coincidence of my little brother Jamie now going to his school and fall into my arms after all. (No. Stupid thought.)*

Really Quite Bad Things About School

1. *Everyone is talking about Claudia's major fifteenth birthday party next week (to which all her older, Year-Eleven-type friends are invited – but not Poppy and me).*
2. *A simple 'Who Is The Most Tanned?' contest ended up in a big argument. During the judging (based on the classic Watch Strap Test), Claudia said Sasha couldn't really be in the contest because she was*

black and Sasha got upset and called her racist, and it all got very
complicated, and we had to stop.

3. *Poppy showed everyone her Danny photos and you could see the*
   wigwams in the background, so Claudia now knows our holiday was
   Not Very Glamorous.

Then, last thing on Friday we heard on the grapevine that there was a Boy Outside One Of The School Gates, and it was Luke.

Luke, outside school waiting for Lorraine!

Ouch, ouch, ouch.

Poppy, Sasha and I saw that it was him at roughly the same moment, and they simultaneously moved either side of me for protection. Bethan and Charlotte saw him and went 'Phwoargh!' and everything, and Sasha told them to shut up. I love Poppy and Sasha. Luke was in his school uniform, holding a big art folder decorated with really good squiggles. I really wanted Luke to meet *me* after school. Did Lorraine even appreciate it?

As Poppy, Sasha and I walked past, with me sandwiched in the middle, a mad old bloke started following us along the road, lurching from side to side and shouting nonsense!

I looked around and unfortunately met Luke's gaze as he walked behind Nutty Bloke with Lorraine. I noticed Lorraine had got changed into her own clothes. Poppy turned too and grinned briefly at them, so I forced myself to smile too. I had the splitting-in-two feeling again.

Luke raised an eyebrow in Nutty Bloke's direction (now miming obscene acts using an empty can of beer as a prop) as if to say, 'Who's your new friend?'

As usual Lorraine just stared over, expressionless. She put her hand through his arm, then looked at me as if to reinforce that she was the one who was with him. It was official then – Lorraine was a boy magnet and what was I? A nutter magnet.

The Chamber of Secrets

On Saturday night I went to sleep over at Poppy's. She promptly decided we would sneak into Luke's room while he was out working late!

'Why?'

'Because we can,' she said, emerging from the under-stairs cupboard covered in dust. 'He doesn't even know there are spare keys here. Ha!'

She let us into Luke's room and quietly shut the door behind us. I looked round at this mysterious space. I had never been in there before. And I had no idea what was behind Poppy's sudden urge to explore. Luke's art folder was there, propped up against the wall. So was his guitar, which looked like it had been gathering dust recently. I went over to his shelves. Oh, he had that book called *The Time Out Film Guide*, which I wanted too!

'Look,' said Poppy, holding up a *Highway Code* booklet on his desk. 'He's going to learn to drive as soon as he's seventeen. Trying to impress Lorraine.'

'How's it going with them?' I asked. I sat down on the bed, in readiness. It made me feel sick, but I preferred to ask rather than wait to be told.

'Fine,' said Poppy, but in an odd voice.

'Fine?' I echoed. I hoped that she was going to say, 'Actually they hate each other and he's out right now buying you roses. The flower kind AND the chocolate kind.'

There was a silence, and then Poppy said really quietly, 'He gave her all his blackcurrant Starbursts!'

'What?'

'He bought Starbursts. He used to give *me* the blackcurrant ones because he doesn't like them. But he came in with Lorraine and they stood in the kitchen and he gave them all to *her*!'

I think she was trying to say he wasn't happy with Lorraine! I was delighted. I pulled a Very Sympathetic face, while suppressing an alluring mental image of Lorraine exploding messily after too many blackcurrant Starbursts, and Luke falling into my arms.

'And then when Mum and Dad were out,' Poppy hissed vehemently, 'she lit up a cigarette *in our hall!*'

'Oh dear,' I said supportively – Poppy's house always smelled of air freshener. I decided not to remind her of Danny's nicotine habit.

'And Luke was being an IDIOT. He told me to keep out of their way and go to my room!' Poppy sounded like she couldn't decide whether to be tearful or furious. 'And I know he's trying to impress her by pretending he's into the same music as her. As if.'

'What kind of music?'

'Oh, you know, really awful, loud dance music. What an idiot. He's downloaded all this new stuff.'

Poppy showed me the new music on his MP3 player. The

albums were all called stuff like, 'Clubbing Anthems 3'.

'I must give him my cousin Will's DJ-ing CD,' I said. I told myself I was helping Will's CD reach his intended audience – you know, rather than just getting rid of it.

'Which A-levels did Lorraine choose?' I asked, changing the subject. It just felt like Luke and I had lots of stuff in common. His A-levels had nearly all been things I'd choose. It didn't seem fair that we weren't together. But maybe I was wrong? Perhaps Lorraine had those things in common with him, too?

'I don't know,' said Poppy shortly. 'He doesn't tell me anything any more.'

Despite their superficial disagreements, Poppy and Luke used to be really close. Which explained why Poppy was now sneaking into his room to find out what he was up to. Ugh, though. I didn't like the thought of Luke being private about Lorraine. As I looked around the room, I saw a used pair of cinema tickets on his desk, to an 18-rated film! I don't know why that surprised me. I guess I had just never actually thought about Luke getting in to see 18s already, and presumably paying for Lorraine. He didn't have tons of cash, did he? Either way, it made their relationship seem depressingly real. I realised they had moments I would never know about. It was obvious, but it struck me how distant I was from him. Even though I was sat on his stripy duvet cover, sur-rounded by his film posters. There was nothing in his room connected to me, even remotely. Nothing to give me hope that I featured somewhere on his landscape. I sighed and carefully switched off Luke's MP3 player so he wouldn't know we'd been in his room.

'It's smelly in here,' declared Poppy, suddenly cottoning on and trying to make me feel better. 'Socks, and . . .'

'Lynx aftershave,' I said glumly.

So we went into Poppy's room and blocked the light from round her door with her bath towel so no one could tell we were going to stay up really late. Then we put sun cream on our arms and smelled it with our eyes closed, so we could pretend we were still at camp, while Poppy talked about Danny and The Kiss.

French was the second-to-last lesson on Friday and I needed it to recover from cross-country. Firstly, I had chickened out of delivering my excuse (risk of exploding if I went above five miles an hour). So Jo had tried to strengthen our resolve with the observation that running was just walking but in fast-forward, but we still came joint last. And there were loads of random old blokes out walking their dogs in Cameron Park – you'd think they'd steer clear when we were all monopolising the place.

Also, why did I choose German GCSE? Clearly a huge mistake. In the morning's lesson, two deeply unnerving things had become clear:

a) *German is really hard.*

b) *All the cool people chose Spanish.*

I fought back the nagging worry that I wasn't actually clever at all ('Oh well, with GCSEs she reached her limit!') sat up and tried to listen really hard. I think the problem was that I was really sleepy after cross-country, and our new French teacher, Mme

Tournon, kept trying to teach us stuff which was far too advanced. Mme Tournon was very short and sturdy, with tufty dark hair and glasses that made her eyes look huge. The overall effect was of a demented owl. Today she was giving us a lesson on the difference between totally identical-sounding vowels.

'*Dessus* means above,' she said. '*Dessous* means below. *Répétez!*'

We all chanted the words, exchanging uneasy glances. They sounded identical. The trouble was that Mme Tournon was a real, live French person, whereas our previous French teacher had been from Milton Keynes.

'*Dessous* is *oo*. But *dessus* is *oo*.' said Mme Tournon firmly. 'Oo, oo.'

'Oo, oo,' we repeated dutifully, everyone but Sasha resisting the temptation to do an owl impression.

'*Non!*'

Mme Tournon was obviously failing to grasp that we didn't even understand accents yet and just put them everywhere at random. We were unlikely to master the subtleties of French pronunciation.

Suddenly I had a major breakthrough moment, which shook off my sleepiness. Unfortunately it wasn't inspired by 'oo' versus 'oo', but the thought that I could organise a party for my fifteenth birthday in October, just like Claudia's! That would be so cool! Why hadn't I thought of it before? There were so many types of party to choose from:

The Illicit House Party: *held in a huge mansion while parents are away, leading to unparalleled snogging opportunities in bedrooms, lots of drinking of violently-coloured jelly vodka shots (or possibly*

*punch), followed by a rapid scramble to tidy up before parents
return home early.*

I had to dismiss this one due to living in a suburban terrace rather than a Californian mansion, not being old enough to buy vodka, and my parents never leaving me alone, ever. What about a party in an Über-Cool venue instead?

Party in an Über-Cool Venue:

Where everyone sees you arrive casually in a Ferrari and you have an immensely cool band play live. (As illustrated in the kind of MTV show where they follow around a rich teenager planning her party.)

This option was also tricky, though – because I could just imagine the TV crew from MTV doing their filming:

(MTV presenter with big microphone): 'Let's start with an impressive, sweeping camera shot of Holly's swimming pool, pampered pets, home cinema, etc. OK, well that was . . . er, quick! Is there anything in this house apart from sporting equipment? Never mind, let's follow Holly in her hunt for an amazing couture dress in, er . . . H&M. And is this a fawning friend begging to be invited? Oh – no. That is just Holly's little brother, speaking in a strange accent. Well, let's move on to her parents, doubtless promising Holly celebrity bands and illicit liquor. What's that Mr Stockwell? Er, sorry . . . no, I don't know how to play golf.'

I shared my ideas with Poppy on the bus home, while stapling back on the handles of my TopShop bag. (And it was getting crumpled, too. Can you iron TopShop bags?) Poppy felt my ideas were good but possibly a bit difficult to organise. She suggested the third option of fancy dress, but we rejected this fairly quickly, as fancy-dress parties are all the same (girls wandering around in long dresses trying to look like someone beautiful from a film, and the boys trying to look cool by wearing sunglasses indoors).

When I got home, Mum asked me to the country club AGAIN, so I distracted her by describing my future party. She said fifteen wasn't a special birthday (outrageous!) and we couldn't afford a party.

'You can afford a country club membership,' I pointed out.

'That's for the whole family.'

'But I never use it.'

'That's your decision.'

I stomped upstairs – the wooden stairs leading up to my loft room make a really good noise. Oh, great. Ivy was in my room, on the rowing machine. I sunk face down onto my pillow, before spluttering back upwards.

'Can you die from inhaling feathers?'

'No,' said Ivy. She added unexpectedly, 'What's up? You were upset the other day when Mrs Mastiff was here.'

I picked bits of feather from my mouth. The thing is, Luke kept going round in my head. So I took a deep breath and, for the first time ever, I told Ivy something about my life.

'Oh, *that* girl,' said Ivy in a disdainful tone. She kept rowing. 'The one who flicks her hair all the time.'

I was hugely encouraged. 'Exactly! She's so awful! But it's OK,' I'm being normal with Luke. You know, civil.'

'Go on . . .'

I explained about Sasha's advice. 'You know – it's important that I retain some dignity. I don't want to make a fool of myself. It's good. Everyone's being really supportive.'

'So Luke knows how you feel?' Ivy got up and switched to the exercise bike.

'I told him at camp!' I said, suppressing the memory of the phone call and how awkward he had been. How embarrassing.

'I don't know,' mused Ivy. 'If you don't let him know you still like him, how can you find out what's going on in his head?'

I started to get annoyed. I was explaining the situation, not asking for her advice. Ivy had no idea how raw and vulnerable I had felt when I first saw Luke and Lorraine together! Following Sasha's advice was the best thing to do.

I waited for Ivy to leave so I could slam the door, but she carried on cycling so I stomped downstairs again. With no apparent sense of irony, Ivy called out, 'You'd better not be going in my room!' So I muttered rude things under my breath and went into Jamie's empty bedroom.

I stood looking at the street out of his open window, fuming gently to myself at Ivy's stupid opinions. How come universities hadn't gone back yet? Ivy was leaving next weekend but only temporarily, to take part in a triathlon (whatever that was). Couldn't she just stay up there all term? Or better still, forever?

Secondly, the Luke thing was getting to me. I used to think you could be honest and not conceal things. But that felt like a long time ago. Everyone I knew had said I'd been weak letting Luke know how I felt. They were right – it had really backfired! Ivy was wrong.

I was still staring at the street when I had to duck suddenly because Luke and Lorraine were walking up the road! They paused just beyond my house while Lorraine lit a cigarette. I crouched below Jamie's window, pulling a face in their direction.

'. . . at this club in London,' Lorraine was saying.

Bleurgh. To cheer myself up, I sucked my cheeks in and looked haughty (a commendable Lorraine impression), then flicked my hair and nearly concussed myself on the base of the window frame. Ouch.

'What's the night called again?' said Luke.

'Strobe5000. It's, like, all one word.'

'Great!' said Luke, after a doubtful-sounding pause.

'Mind you, you'll need some decent clothes,' said Lorraine. 'You won't be able to wear old trainers. Or your school uniform!'

She laughed lightly as if she wasn't really having a dig at him. Scandal! Luke was gorgeous whatever he had on.

'Right. OK,' said Luke hesitantly.

'Can you drive me and my mates?' asked Lorraine. There was a pause, then she continued, 'You don't mind if they come too, do you?'

'It's not that,' said Luke. 'I don't drive, not yet. You have to be seventeen to learn.'

'Oh, yes. Of course. Sorry.'

I wondered how many people she had gone out with who could drive. Quite a few, clearly.

Suddenly I was interrupted.

'Holly, what are you doing?' said Jamie's voice, right in my ear.

I yelped in surprise and clamped my hand over my mouth so no more noise would come out. My professional surveillance had been going so well!

'Nobody, I mean, nothing,' I told Jamie, the words muffled through my fingers. Two boys, presumably Asif and Imran, were smirking in the doorway to Jamie's room. A meerkat-style peer out of the window confirmed that Luke and Lorraine didn't seem to have heard, but it cost me three bars of Dairy Milk for Jamie to promise not to yell through the open window, 'Holly's spying on you!' Was this what my life had come to – crouching on my hands and knees eavesdropping on Luke and being blackmailed by a bunch of eleven-year-olds?

Psycho

Mental note: You can't iron TopShop bags.

I don't know why my mum was so annoyed about a few tiny bits of plastic stuck on the iron. When Poppy was six, she burned an iron-shaped hole in her parents' brand new carpet trying to straighten her Barbie doll's hair! Well, she claimed she was six, I bet she was actually nine.

I escaped round to Poppy's. She was on her way out to London. 'Want to come?' she asked.

'Maybe. I don't feel like going home. Apparently I am a danger to unattended household appliances.'

I wearily watched Poppy take off her T-shirt and her pair of fluffy slippers, and replace them with a black long-sleeved top and her black boots.

Then she got out her eyeliner, frowned and said, 'This is melting in this heat.'

It was so clear she was forcing herself to put it on!

'Why don't you just go out in your normal stuff?' I said bravely.

Or stupidly, depending on your point of view.

Poppy gave me a Look and pointed meaningfully at her furry slippers. 'What, in those?'

'You know what I mean! Just show him *you*.'

'This is me,' said Poppy unconvincingly, doing up her boots.

I looked away and fed Mouse a Choc Treat. His fur looked a bit tufty, like he hadn't been expecting visitors. I thought, 'Poppy, this is not you – it's a ridiculous façade you are putting on for Danny.'

Poppy sighed, interpreting my silence. 'Look Holly, this is about expressing my individuality. You know, being distinctive, rising above the average.'

What did that mean? Was I average?

Poppy must have seen my face because she backtracked a bit and attempted kindly, 'Not everybody has to be . . . distinctive and original.'

Which was funny, because she looked just like Danny!

'I don't think I'll come along today,' I said, probably to our mutual relief. We walked down the road together as far as my house, then I went inside.

'What are you doing back?' said Mum as I stepped through the door.

'Poppy is out for the afternoon.'

'So you're around?' said Mum, sounding strangely animated.

'Er – no?' I said rapidly, sensing I'd made a tactical error.

'But you just said you were!'

'No – honestly – I need to stay here and pick plastic off the iron.'

Five minutes later, I was being bundled out of the house and into the car with Jamie, who promptly leaped in the front seat so I was stuck in the back, like the younger child. Drat.

Mum drove us to the country club and signed in while I looked in vain for either reading material or a vending machine.

'I'm sure you'll both do very well!' said the woman behind the counter, a bit oddly. She added, 'The changing rooms are over there.'

I didn't get properly suspicious until Mum steered me to a discreet spot beside a big pot plant and pressed a bag into my hand. It contained my trainers and school purple and grey PE kit!

'It'll be fun!' she said, ominously.

'What will?'

'The Mother-Daughter Sports Day.'

I looked at her in silence, until Jamie attracted my attention by practically wetting himself with laughter.

'You knew about this?' I said, furiously.

'Hahahahahaha!'

Jamie KEPT doing this to me. I had been nice. I had taken him on the bus. And how had he repaid me? First blackmailing me for chocolate and now this! It was war!

'No,' I told Mum. 'Absolutely not.'

'What do you expect me to do? Ivy's doing her triathlon this weekend!'

'Put a wig on Jamie!' I said, aghast.

We stared at each other while I tried hard to think of a way out. I knew there wasn't one. Although maybe I had been inspired by the demanding teenagers on MTV, because I attempted one thing.

'If I do this, can I have a birthday party?'

OK, so I sounded like that spoiled one from *Charlie and the*

114

Chocolate Factory. But Jamie and the woman behind the counter looked quite impressed.

'No!' Mum snorted.

OK, extortion wasn't really my style. I went and got ready in the changing rooms alongside lots of other mothers and daughters, silently wishing I was feisty like Sasha. It was mad – the other daughters all looked like they actually wanted to be there! I guess Mum and I look similar enough to the outside world, but on the inside we have nothing in common.

Mum looked at me in my PE kit and said, 'You'll do.' I knew she would have preferred it if I had been Ivy. I guess everyone has their disappointments in life. 'Oh well,' she continued, 'Vanessa will be thrilled we're taking part, anyway.'

'Vanessa Sheringham?'

'She's our celebrity sponsor!' said Mum proudly.

Great. If Vanessa Sheringham was there, then so was Claudia.

I read once that sometimes your brain blanks out stressful events. Well, all I remember of the actual sporting events was Vanessa and Claudia excelling effortlessly at the egg and spoon race. I did *try* – I moved and stuff. I didn't want to let Mum down, but I think I simply lack the gene for moving fast. Whenever I think about speeding up, my legs go, 'Why?' Fortunately Mum kept letting Vanessa win, so she didn't push me too much.

My clearest memory is of drinks on the veranda afterwards. I went to the Ladies and got back to find Mum had parked herself next to Vanessa and Claudia, and was unsuccessfully trying to

115

engage Vanessa in conversation.

'Of course, Holly might start coming here for the yoga,' she was saying, as I sat down.

We all watched Vanessa work up the botheredness to formulate a reply. Maybe she didn't want to use her facial muscles unnecessarily in case of wrinkling? Or maybe she'd had Botox and couldn't register much emotion on her face.

'Claudia found the lessons weren't very good,' Vanessa managed finally. 'We got her a private instructor in the end.'

'Maybe we'll do that too,' said Mum valiantly.

'They are rather expensive,' said Vanessa. Outrageous! It is OK for me to be irritated by my mum, but not other people. Even Claudia looked embarrassed.

'And my husband George might start coming here for the golf,' said Mum.

Oh God, I thought, please let's not mention Claudia's dad. Since the divorce he lived in an apartment in Kensington and bought Claudia expensive presents, while Vanessa now had a boyfriend who was younger than she was.

There was no response at all from Vanessa. In desperation, Mum changed the subject. 'And of course it's nice that Claudia and Holly are friends!'

Everyone else looked less than enchanted with this description. Vanessa nudged her shades down her nose with one manicured finger, looked me up and down in my school PE kit and said doubtfully, 'Did I see you on the list for Claudia's fifteenth birthday party?'

'I couldn't make it,' I said, gazing straight at Claudia. She had the grace to look away.

'Well, then,' said Mum jovially, 'Claudia will have to come to Holly's party, instead. We might have that here!'

What?

Mum saw my expression and continued hastily, 'It'll just be a small thing, of course, but you're only fifteen once, after all! Not like us old souls!'

Vanessa took a big gulp of her white wine and pushed her shades back back, distinctly unimpressed at being referred to as an old soul. Mum finally shut up and looked hesitantly at me. I smiled serenely back.

'It'll just be something small,' Mum said again while we were changing. 'And I doubt it will be on the actual day because of the short notice.'

Brilliant.

'And we can't have it here – it will cost too much.'

'That's fine,' I said serenely. A sports venue was the last place I wanted for my party, anyway. I was sure the Hard Rock Café had a section you could reserve for parties – or we could go to an under-Eighteens' night in a cool club?

'I know – the badminton court in the sports hall is sometimes free.'

The badminton court? What, in the crummy local sports hall? For my party?

'We can bring a CD player and Jenga and team games too! Ooh, and Auntie Valerie could leave the net up, so people can play. And I could do some food – you know, carrot sticks and dips.'

She looked up and clearly mistook the panic on my face for the fear of a chocolate-free night, because she conceded, 'And maybe a cake.'

Suddenly we were interrupted, by Claudia of all people! She came over to me and asked, 'Can I have a word?'

Trying to figure out why Claudia was saving me from Mum's party ideas, I followed her over to a deserted corner of the changing room. It was hard to keep up in one shoe and one grey and purple sock.

'I want to make up with Poppy,' said Claudia bluntly. 'You can help me.'

Oh my God!

'But she's still upset about Jez!'

'I split up with Jez,' said Claudia. 'Yesterday.' She looked at me hopefully, as if this might be the key to reconciliation.

Oh my God. Weirdly, my first feeling was relief that now the feud could be over.

'Because of Poppy!' I exclaimed. Wow – Claudia had a conscience after all!

'Well, no, not really,' said Claudia honestly. 'I, er – met someone else at camp. Mark. Seventeen. Windsurfing instructor.'

'But that was ages ago!'

'Er – yes.'

'Oh,' I said. So, Claudia had stolen Jez from Poppy and then two-timed him!

Considering that the last time Claudia and Poppy were friends, they had gone off without me and made my life a misery, I could have easily refused to help. Not to mention that Claudia had nearly ruined my life trying to go off with Luke! But then again, everyone would be happier if this was sorted out. It was pretty miserable, everyone being enemies. And there was some annoying part of me that wanted her approval. At least if I helped, then Claudia might think I was cool!

'OK, I'll try,' I said.

Claudia beamed, and then, sounding like the big, burly one out of *The Sopranos*, she said fiercely, 'But don't tell her I asked you. This is not something I do every day.'

How could there be homework to do when I had the party and the Claudia Situation to think about? And why did I choose really hard GCSE subjects with lots of work and thinking involved, rather than easy stuff like crafts and media studies?

Poppy called me late that evening. 'I'm back from London,' she announced. 'It was cool. Are you doing the trigonometry homework?'

See? She *did* care about school.

'Just finished it,' I replied.

'I started, but then I discovered a new way to eat Maltesers. You stick them on the end of a compass and dunk them in tea. It's brilliant.'

I told Poppy about the sports day and then the party, which made her forget momentarily about the Maltesers.

'Brilliant!' she exclaimed. 'I can bring Danny and we can go off somewhere and snog!'

'Well – yes – but, I don't know – what about my mum? She'll never allow me to invite boys!'

'You have to have boys. It's a party!'

'Not in My-Mum-World, you don't. She's talking about Jenga and badminton!'

I heard pensive Malteser-slurping noises. 'Look,' Poppy said eventually, 'don't worry about that. When will your mum have finished setting up?'

'I don't know. About seven?'

'We'll just tell the boys it starts at eight. Let her plan the party her way and then, once she's gone, we'll just replace the Jenga and shuttlecocks with Spin the Bottle like at normal parties.'

'Poppy? What if no one comes?'

'You are ridiculous. Of course people will come!'

'I'm scared now. I didn't think it would actually happen. I don't even know that many boys!'

'You know, er . . . a few. Well, Sasha does, doesn't she?'

I took a deep breath. 'What if I invited Claudia? She knows lots of boys.'

Poppy audibly choked on a half-melted Malteser.

I retold the story about Claudia and Jez, omitting only that Claudia had asked for me to help them be friends again.

Poppy said 'Ha!' and then went quiet.

'So, I guess you'll make up with Claudia now?' I said.

'What, after what she did?'

I got the first stirrings of dread. Oh God, was Poppy *not* going to forgive Claudia? I hadn't actually expected this. If Poppy was still angry, would that be my fault?

'Aren't things different now?' I asked, panicked.

'Nothing's changed! She still went off with him. If anything, she's shown it didn't even mean that much in the first place. But

120

it was enough to chuck in our friendship for!'

Wow. She was really angry.

'And she was horrible about me having black hair.'

Urk. Clearly I was treading on eggshells myself, in that respect.

'You used to be really good friends,' I persisted, not quite sure what I was trying to say. It just seemed a bit . . . harsh! It was clear Claudia was making an effort, which she didn't need to do, so Poppy's friendship obviously meant something to her. And, if Poppy was rebuffing her just out of pride, then it all seemed a bit sad and unnecessary.

On Monday in history, Claudia sat down in front of us, turned and smiled tentatively at Poppy. Poppy didn't smile back.

'Aren't you going to talk to her ever again?' I wrote to Poppy on my rough book.

Poppy snorted and underlined where I had written *Dignity is Key* with her biro. Then she said out loud, 'She can sod off.'

Claudia's shoulders tensed up.

I opened my mouth but Mrs Constance arrived, so instead I wrote down the date of the party in big letters on my rough book and nudged Poppy.

'How come it's a week late?' scrawled Poppy next to it.

I risked a whisper. 'Mum's badminton club booked the hall on my actual birthday weekend. Don't ask.'

'But surely she could —' Poppy's voice rose in outrage.

'I know. Don't say it.' Mum had said the hall was booked over my actual birthday weekend for a monthly badminton tournament and the date couldn't be changed. When I'd asked about it, it turned out it was Mum's own team using the hall!

I lowered my voice to an Extreme Whisper so Claudia definitely wouldn't hear. 'Mum wouldn't even be letting me have a party, if it wasn't for trying to impress you-know-who's mum.'

'Shh!' said Mrs Constance. I hoped it was a non-specific, whole-class-type 'Shush', but she was looking right at me.

We went quiet while Mrs Constance started on about 'The Great Question of the Russian Revolution', whatever that was. History had got harder too. Poppy and I were a bit lost so we started a list on a spare bit of paper:

Great Questions of Life

1. *Why do buses never turn up when you need one?*
2. *Why in magazines do they always chop up lipsticks that cost fifteen pounds when they could take a normal photo of them and then keep them? Does a beauty editor then mash them up into little pots or do they chuck them out?*

We passed it to Charlotte and Bethan, who added some more questions and passed it back:

3. *Why in French are things like tables masculine or feminine when they clearly aren't either?*
4. *Why do you never see baby pigeons?*
5. *Why did we choose history GCSE?*

At the end of the lesson, Claudia turned and said to Poppy, 'So, did Holly tell you? Jez and I split up!'

'She told me,' said Poppy in a tight voice. 'I heard you were two-timing him with some guy called Mark?'

Claudia glanced at me, and I felt a funny sense of dread in my stomach. I had told Poppy that, of course, because it was part of the story. But it sounded as if I hadn't been trying to help.

'Not two-timing exactly,' Claudia said sharply, 'more . . . slightly overlapping.'

'Oh – *overlapping*,' said Poppy, dripping sarcasm. She looked away and blinked a bit, which was when I realised she was actually quite upset. But determined not to show it.

Blimey. All this and it was only Monday. A whole week until another weekend!

Claudia silently packed up her stuff and walked away, turning only to glare. But it wasn't Poppy she glared at. It was me.

From Rush Hour With Love

I am clearly rubbish at getting out of things. I ended up doing a second cross-country run that Wednesday!

I really couldn't be bothered to run, and neither could Jo, so we sat behind a bush in a remote spot halfway round the course. We chatted and agreed that cross-country needed a bit more of an incentive, like chocolate at the end, or a special offer like 'Run this one, get out of the next one'. We waited for the others to almost come back round, then re-joined the circuit just in front of them. We hadn't thought it through very well, however, because Mrs Mastiff didn't notice we'd missed a circuit and thought we had come first!

I went home in my PE kit, thinking dejectedly about Mrs. Mastiff's new plans to enter Jo and I in the next inter-school championship. How was I going to get out of the team now?

By the time I reached home I was so deep in thought that I nearly missed Luke walking past on the other side of the road! On his own, thank God.

'Holly!' he said and waved hello.

'Hold on a minute,' I told him. 'I keep forgetting to give you something.' I opened the front door and pegged it upstairs for Will's CD. When I got back, Luke was hovering in my front garden, looking up at the porch.

'Look, Holly —' he begun.

Oh God, he was going to give me a talk about how our kiss hadn't meant anything. It was just too humiliating. Plus I was standing there like an idiot in a purple and grey PE kit, with muddy bits on my bottom from sitting behind the bush. So I spared us both.

'I was just getting this for you,' I interrupted, handing him the CD. 'It's my cousin Will's. He does dance music. Poppy told me you'd started listening to stuff like this.'

Luke slowly turned it over in his hand, then said, 'Thanks.'

'How was the film the other day?' I asked. Then I remembered I'd seen the tickets in his room and lied hastily, 'Poppy mentioned you'd seen it. It got really good reviews.'

'Um, yes – it was . . . fine.'

Pause. Then I steeled myself for a big one.

'You and Lorraine must come to my party,' I said.

There you go. If that wasn't the ultimate don't-care gesture, what was? But he didn't even want to, I could tell! He sort of went, 'Well – yes, er, maybe. Thank you.'

God, acting nonchalant was hard when it was just the two of us and there was no one around to draw encouraging gold stars on available surfaces. And we were back at my house, under the porch he had stood on to kiss me. I wondered if he even remembered. I had been so optimistic. It felt like a long time ago.

'Who was that?' said Mum, as I shut the door after he'd left.

'No one,' I said.

On Thursday after school, Poppy and I went window shopping. There was so much nice, new autumn-type stuff, it was unreal! As usual I couldn't afford very much in TopShop. It wasn't fair. I wanted another bag!

I sighed. 'Do you think they would give me a large bag for a tiny hair clip, if I asked nicely?'

'I tried once,' said Poppy. 'Didn't work.'

I looked around for something bulky but not expensive. Eventually I managed to find a scarf reduced in the sale, but when I paid for it the assistant squeezed it into a tiny, thin, useless small bag! There should be trading standards outlawing that kind of behaviour. Poppy steered me away from the scene of this crime into Accessorize and planned the party for me.

'OK, we invite boys and just hide the Jenga and the team games,' said Poppy, starting a list on her phone. 'Boys. Who do we know?'

'Luke,' I started. 'But he doesn't want to come.'

'OK, not Luke. Right – there's Danny and his friend Matt, Sam from camp, Stephen . . .'

'Would Stephen come?'

'Dunno. Don't think he likes us. Well, not you, because you didn't want to do his horse-riding. But Sam will come and Stephen's his neighbour, so you never know. Besides, he's seventeen and quite good-looking.'

We pondered this for a minute. It would look cool that we

knew him. So we kept him on the list. But there still weren't enough boys. What if it was just me, Poppy and a game of Jenga in the middle of an empty hall?

'What about Pritesh?' said Poppy.

'What, the newsagent's son? I think he's gone to uni. Dentistry.'

'Or . . . that bloke on the bus?'

'What, Stripy Scarf boy? The one we don't actually know and have never spoken to?'

'Yes,' Poppy admitted.

There was a pause.

'OK,' I continued, 'Girls. Tess, Rachel, Sasha . . . Jo can only come for the start because it's her Dad's birthday . . . shall I invite Claudia?'

Poppy gave me a look that meant, 'Are you mad?'

I tried again. 'Look, Poppy – Claudia really wants to make things up. You know, she really wants to be friends with you again. It's important to her.'

'Oh, really?'

'Yes – look – she even asked if I could help.'

OK, I know I'd said I wouldn't mention it, but it was definitely my best shot to show that Claudia cared!

Poppy scowled fiercely at a poor, innocent hair clip that happened to be on the display in front of her. 'She is so sneaky!'

'But —'

'What, she thinks she can get to me by talking to my best friend behind my back?'

Poppy picked up the clip and firmly put it back down in completely the wrong place, as if that would show the universe not to mess with her.

God, I wished there was a textbook for these situations.

'We need to think of lots of good games,' I said, switching back to the safer subject of party planning as we made our way into River Island.

'Twister!' said Poppy.

'Obviously.'

'Chess!' said Poppy.

'Chess is pointless. It involves no physical contact with boys whatsoever.'

'Lemons,' said a nearby security guard, which was a bit odd.

I discreetly pulled a face at Poppy. See? I was a Nutter Magnet.

'The Lemon Game,' the security guard elaborated. 'You get a lemon under your chin and have to pass it to the next person with your hands behind your back.'

We looked at him with new-found respect. 'Thank you!' said Poppy, impressed. We added it to our list.

'So – this party venue. Is there a bedroom for snogging in?' said Poppy, lowering her voice.

'I told you, it's a sports hall.'

'So . . .?'

'So, no bedrooms.'

'Any kind of room?'

'I don't know. I've only ever been in there to sit on the side-lines. When forced.' I thought harder as we left River Island and headed for the bus stop home. 'There's a cloakroom, I think. Near the entrance. It's got a coat rail and some footballs in it.'

'That'll do.'

I noticed during the usual ten-billion-hour wait for a bus home that Poppy was back to using her old schoolbag again – the brown

128

leather one she'd had last year.

Poppy saw me looking. 'I'm just using this one today because the handle broke on the black one. I do like my black bag.'

'I've got a stapler you can borrow if you like,' I said as we finally got on a bus, to show I was agreeing with her.

As we sat down upstairs Poppy jabbed me in the side and hissed, 'There! Stripy Scarf Boy. Behind us. Why don't you try fancying him?'

As if you could just decide to move on? I turned to look. He was just a random boy. It was like when all you had to eat was cooking chocolate. You could try to pretend, but it just wasn't the real thing.

'He's nothing special.'

'You mean, he's not Luke,' said Poppy annoyingly.

At that point, my phone rang. I reached into my bag but, weirdly, the screen looked like this:

Calling: Poppy mobile

'Your phone has called my number by mistake,' I said to Poppy, puzzled.

She leaned closer to me so her mouth was by my ear. 'Answer it!'

'Er, OK.' I hit the button. 'Hello?'

Unsurprisingly, all I could hear was Poppy's stuff moving round in her bag where the phone was on.

'There's no one there,' I said to her in a slow voice normally reserved for very small children. I pressed the 'End Call' button.

'You're useless!' hissed Poppy. 'I was giving you the opportunity to chat and laugh loudly and stuff, so you looked really popular in front of that boy!'

I wondered if I would ever catch on to this relationship thing, with all the pretending and games. Probably not.

That's when we saw Luke and Lorraine come up the bus stairs! This time Luke had got changed out of his school uniform – and it looked as if he had just spent a fortune on clothes, because he was holding lots of shopping bags! He could wave goodbye to his earnings from this summer, then. I felt my heart plummet. He obviously really, really liked Lorraine if he was willing to spend the cash from his summer job to please her.

I noticed Lorraine was holding a pile of textbooks – economics and business studies. See. All wrong! Then, while sashaying down the aisle behind Luke, Lorraine ran her hand through her hair and flicked it back!

'Why does she do that?' I asked scathingly.

With that, Poppy took my breath away.

'She's all right, you know,' she said calmly, as if this was a completely normal thing to fling at your best friend.

'But —' I spluttered. 'You —'

'She came round the other day and she was really nice.'

Shock, horror!

'But you said you hated her!' I gasped, feeling betrayed.

'She said my hair was cool – she reckons this colour is really in at the moment! She's not a horrible person – she's just got Luke and you haven't.'

I couldn't believe it. Surely the one thing you should be able to count on is your friends being supportive and disliking the same people as you?

'You have got to get over Luke,' said Poppy. 'Just have a laugh! Snog some random people!'

130

'How come you're suddenly bugging me about this?'

'Sasha and I agreed you needed to!'

Oh great. Sasha doesn't usually hang out with Poppy, but now they were clubbing together to tell me I was mad?

It was quite funny when we all lined up waiting to go downstairs for our stop. The letter *L* had fallen from the local public hall, so that it read *Pubic Hall*. I nudged Poppy and we both got the giggles. Lorraine sniffed and rolled her eyes as if I was really immature. But Luke grinned too – ha!

Then Luke and I went to ring the bell at the same time and he accidentally put his hand on mine! It was totally electric. He looked straight at me. It all happened so fast I had no idea what expression was on my face. Then he withdrew his hand really quickly. I would have liked to think he'd done it on purpose, but my instincts hadn't been very accurate so far.

The next day, I complained to Sasha about Poppy's betrayal over Lorraine and she said annoyingly, 'It sounds like she's just telling you what you've told her about Claudia.'

I don't think people should be allowed to point out uncomfortable truths to you on your birthday. Why does everyone have to be honest, anyway? I'd found the best way with Luke was to pretend, after all!

It was a brilliant birthday, though, even with my party not being until the following weekend. Fifteen! I can see Fifteen-rated films at the cinema! I remember when I thought that was really old. But with a bit more perspective I can see that it isn't, not really. Not like being twenty-five or anything like that. I got six cards in the post before school: one from Grandma Stockwell and one from Grandma Bradshaw (both posies of flowers), a card with balloons on from Auntie Anne and Uncle Grant, with a paw print drawn on it in biro from their dog and a big 'X' from Will (a signature, I think, rather than a kiss), and a fab card from Tess with a pink furry rim.

Mum, Dad, Jamie and Ivy clubbed together to give me some birthday money and a four-person voucher for ice-skating, which everyone knew I would give to them. But the birthday money was great! Now I could go back to TopShop and buy lots of stuff!

'I want a birthday,' said Jamie disconsolately, eyeing the chocolate that had accompanied Tess's card.

'People should have two birthdays, so the presents are spread out evenly through the year,' I said. 'I think the Queen does that.'

'One a year is enough,' said Dad, taking away the envelopes. 'You stop telling people about your birthday when you get to my age.'

'You can have some chocolate if you promise not to be annoying any more,' I told Jamie, feeling generous.

'What do you mean?' said Jamie cautiously.

'Stop speaking in that fake accent.'

He paused and then said 'OK.' In his normal voice!

Hurrah. I split the chocolate between us. He promptly licked his bit so I wouldn't take it back. Gross!

'It's all slimy now!' I said. 'Like a . . . a slug's walked on it or something!'

'Slugs don't walk, they slither. Ooh, and my accent's coming back . . .! Listen!' He tried to think of something to say, then managed, 'I'm Spider-Man!'

Aargh. Could he get any more annoying?

'Slugman, perhaps,' I retorted. Ha!

Then at school I got lots of other presents. It was a great surprise – I felt really popular. Poppy gave me a really nice card with sequins on it and wrote inside in silver pen that my present was a surprise, due in the next few days.

'Luke wrapped in a big red bow?' I said lightly.

'Not quite . . . sorry.'

Sasha bought me some delicious chocolates from Thorntons and Jo gave me a really nice hair clip from Accessorize and (in a gesture of true friendship) the bag too!

But then on Sunday, when Poppy and I went shopping to spend my riches, there was nothing good in the shops! Nothing! I knew it. The Inverse Shopping Law had taken effect:

The Inverse Shopping Law

* *No money to spend: tons of stuff you want to buy.*
* *Tons of money to spend: nothing at all you want to buy.*

It was crazy. TopShop had one OK-ish white top, but they only had a size six or a size eighteen. Poppy found one on the floor in the right size, but it was price-tag-less and had big foundation smears on it.

'Never mind,' Poppy said, suddenly looking at her watch. 'Follow me!'

'What for?'

She led me into and into Claire's Accessories. Apparently, it was time for my birthday present.

Girl with a Belly-Button Ring

Oh my God. Holes in ears. Definitely not there before. That night, as I stared in my bedroom mirror, I was hugely grateful that my hair covered my ears. But Mum and Dad were still bound to notice at some point. More to the point, what was Poppy going to tell her mum? She had got her belly-button pierced, which was definitely more major!

Although, there was a breakthrough moment in the shop. The piercist was just telling me about how I needed to leave the studs in and twiddle them every night for six weeks when I looked over at Poppy, who was pressing a big lump of cotton wool against her stomach.

'What have you done?' I said, although I could already tell.

She moved the cotton wool silently and I saw a flash of pearl-studded ring surrounded by a livid purple bruise.

'Ugh!'

'It'll go down,' said the piercist, as Poppy blinked back tears of pain.

'Look – Poppy —'

'It just hurts!' she said defensively.

'Look – why are you putting yourself through this? Danny would still like you if you just acted like . . . well, like you.'

'This *is* me. My image is my decision,' said Poppy. But she sounded a bit more feeble than normal. She picked up her bags and I followed her back out into the shopping centre.

'I know, but —'

'It is!'

'It just feels like you're doing this stuff to impress Danny. He would still like you without it, you know.'

'Why are you being mean? I just bought you a present! And now you're acting just like Claudia!'

'I am not!' I gasped.

'Well, she said that too,' muttered Poppy. 'And it's annoying.' She went quiet, then a passer-by bumped into her and she gasped. 'Ouch!'

We walked along in silence.

Finally she said something else.

'I can hardly stop now, can I?'

Oh my God. I could barely believe that I, Holly Stockwell, was right about something!

Poppy frowned at her stomach, then managed, 'He wouldn't still like me.'

I looked at her. 'You don't have to pretend. Danny likes *you*.'

'But I've invested all this time into this! At the start of camp, in my normal stuff, he ignored me. It's easier just to continue.

You're pretending in front of Luke and I don't have a go at you about it!'

'What?'

'Pretending you don't like him!'

She was insane.

'That is *totally* different. That is how I *have* to act. *You* have a choice!'

Poppy poked silently at the dressing.

'Don't touch it. Listen – you have to do something about it. Call him. Or just wear your normal stuff again.'

You could practically see the cogs in Poppy's brain going round. Finally she said, 'I'd like to, but it's gone too far now. It would be far too scary.'

Personally, I thought a big metal thing punching a hole in your stomach was scarier, but we just went back to Poppy's and sat in the kitchen so Poppy could actively conceal her pierced belly button from her mum. I suppressed the usual pang of envy at Poppy's mum, who is lovely and normal and forgives you when you accidentally kill her house plants, never forces you to do Extreme Yoga or Frantic Table Tennis, and lets you make shapes with leftover pastry while she is cooking.

Poppy was making a wigwam shape out of her bit of pastry. She grinned surreptitiously at me and said, 'Mum, can me and Holly go camping again next year?'

'We'll have to wait and see. They do run them every year.'

'Where do you find out about the dates and stuff?' Poppy asked.

Poppy's Mum looked thoughtful. 'Well – Auntie Claire's friend, Malcolm, he runs them. I could just ask him again.'

Malcolm? Poppy's mum sort-of knew Malcolm?

I stared, shocked, at Poppy, who bit her lip to stop herself from laughing.

'He always recommended them as a good way of getting some fresh sea air. His son Daniel goes on every trip.'

I imagined a younger Malcolm with amusement.

'Are you sure?' said Poppy. 'We did notice that, er – there were hardly any boys on ours. And there wasn't anyone called Daniel.'

Then – Oh God.

'Poppy?' I said slowly, 'you know what – we did meet a Danny, didn't we?'

If Poppy's mum had looked up from the pastry, she would have seen an expression of exquisite horror cross her daughter's face.

'NO way,' said Poppy, once we were up in her room. She rocked to and fro at the end of her bed, nervously eating her bit of pastry.

It was true, though. I used my detective skills. We checked there hadn't been any other Daniels on the trip. Then we looked up Danny's landline area code on the Internet and it was a small village in Kent, nowhere near East London! It did explain what someone apparently so cool was doing on an English camping holiday.

'No wonder we got blamed for the smoking!' I said. This explained why the other leaders had let him get away with so much: he was their boss's son!

Poppy wrinkled her nose up. 'What an idiot!' she said in sudden disgust.

When I went home for dinner, Poppy phoned Danny and confronted him!

'Boys!' Poppy exclaimed vehemently down the phone to me later on. You know Storm, the Rottweiler?'

'Yes?'

'His mum's daschund.'

'No way.'

'And Ibiza?'

'Yes?'

'Wales.'

'Oh my God. But what about the clubbing and stuff?'

'Scouts every Sunday afternoon.'

'Nightmare!'

'Do you know what else?' she said in a mortified whisper.

'What?' I said, entranced.

'You know he said he was fifteen?'

'Ye-es.'

'Muurmmeeeeen,' Poppy muttered.

'What?'

'THIRTEEN. HE'S THIRTEEN!'

Oh my God.

'That mate of his, Matt – he looked young because he's thirteen too!'

'Ah,' was the best I could do. Then, 'Why was he pretending?'

'He knows he looks older. I reckon he thought that if he pretended to be fifteen, I would like him more. Though he wouldn't say that. He nearly didn't even tell me the truth! He only confessed in the end because I laughed at him for still going to Scouts.'

Hmm. Danny should have had a warning sign on him – *Compulsive liar, keep clear!* All that time Poppy had been putting on a huge front for Danny, and it turned out he'd been doing the same thing. Oh, and Poppy's parents would probably have been thrilled with her choice of boyfriend. However, I decided not to say this out loud.

There was silence for a moment, then a clunking noise.

'What's that?' I said. It wasn't the sound of Maltesers being dunked into tea.

'Oh, I just kicked my boots into my wardrobe,' said Poppy. 'Right towards the back.'

Then, I couldn't help it. 'Danny Scumton!' I said. And we both started giggling.

Fantastic news! I got reduced to 'probationary status' in the cross-country team, which meant I might get chucked off! That would be such a major achievement. It happened when we were doing yet more running, this time as part of a normal PE lesson. (PE teachers should have more variety in their lessons, I think. Cake-baking, watching MTV, that kind of thing.) Poppy and I stood shivering by the start line in Cameron Park. I tried to cheer her up by reassuring her that Danny looked at least seventeen and that was what counted.

'I told him it was officially over – I couldn't go out with some-one younger,' said Poppy, pulling a face. 'I officially uninvited him and Matt from your party, by the way.'

I nodded in understanding, trying not to think, 'We need more boys!'

'Did you tell Tess?'

'Yes,' said Poppy glumly. 'She sounded relieved, like she'd had a narrow escape. But she was too nice to say so.'

'I could get Jez to come to my party?' I ventured.

Poppy shook her head and crunched an autumn leaf with her trainer. 'Ancient history,' she said, quickly changing the subject. 'What would you rather . . . walk into a big spider's web and for the spider to go in your mouth . . .'

'It would have to be the other thing,' I interrupted, shuddering. 'Nothing could be that bad.'

'Or . . . have a boy you really fancy go into the bathroom after you when it really smells?'

'That's too horrible.'

'You. Have. To. Choose,' said Poppy firmly.

'OK. The spider's web.'

'OK. A nice one. What would you rather . . . free chocolate for life, or to get stuck in a lift with Luke?'

'I might as well go for the chocolate,' I said gloomily. I needed to accept that it just wasn't going to happen with Luke, rather than torturing myself about whether it meant anything when he rang the bell on the bus at the same time as me.

Suddenly Mrs Mastiff let out a bloodcurdling shriek.

'Holly Stockwell!' she bellowed, charging towards me at high speed (surely unsafe in a lesson environment) and coming to rest with her finger pointing at my ear. 'What do you call these?'

'Ears,' I heard Sasha say quietly from somewhere behind me.

'You aren't supposed to take the studs out for six weeks after getting them pierced,' I volunteered bravely.

'And you have to twiddle them,' added Poppy helpfully. We were silenced with a Look.

Five minutes later, as everyone else started running, I was sat by the start line in disgrace, with a note for my parents expressing displeasure that I had failed to remove my earrings for a PE lesson. I was almost fainting with joy. Best of all was Mrs Mastiff's final remark.

'Holly, when I think of how athletic your sister is . . . well. I'm disappointed. And I'm sure your mother will be too. But I won't have people participate in my classes that don't take them seriously. I'll have to consider if you have a future on my cross-country team.'

Pierced ears. The best birthday present ever!

One Party and a Funeral

Honestly, Mum is living in the dark ages. I waited right up until early Friday evening to give her the note (when it would be too late to cancel the party) and she went loopy, demanding to see my ears and giving them more attention than in the entire fifteen years of their existence on the planet to date! I thought it was a bit rich, seeing as I had been walking around with them all week and no one in my family had even noticed, immersed as usual in the country club, Dad's golf and Jamie's football.

'It was a gift from Poppy. You always told me to accept gifts graciously!'

'When did you get this done?'

'Last Sunday.'

'I remember when you couldn't even go to the supermarket on a Sunday, let alone get parts of your body mutilated.'

'Everyone has their ears pierced!' I protested. I couldn't believe it. You see tiny babies in buggies wearing gold studs.

Mum just went, 'Be different!' in this infuriating way. Didn't she realise that normal fifteen-year-olds spend all their time trying to fit in? There's no way I was expending any energy being different.

Ivy was still being annoying. At least I had seen her packing to go back to uni.

'Holly!' she called up the loft stairs. 'Luke's here for you.'

'Very funny,' I yelled. Me and my badly behaved ears had taken refuge in my room. I was eating Hula Hoops off the ends of my fingers, like Jamie and I used to when we were little, and mentally assessing my party plans at the same time. I felt quite optimistic about it, actually. OK, it was in the badminton hall, but we would still have Spin the Bottle and the Lemon Game. And even with the regrettable adjustments to the male headcount (no Danny, no Danny's-friend-Matt), there would still be ten whole boys. OK, they were almost all Sasha's mates who I had never met before, but ten was almost enough to go around!

'No, seriously!'

'Sod off!'

'Language!' cried Mum predictably, from somewhere else in the house.

I stopped crunching and sat still, listening. I could hear Jamie in his room with his friends. But I definitely hadn't heard the doorbell go. And what would Luke be doing here? Then Ivy clomped up the loft stairs.

'Look, you idiot. He's outside. He threw a pebble up to my window. He doesn't know that you switched rooms.'

Oh my God. I scrambled to my feet and tried to straighten my hair in the mirror, then stopped myself abruptly. Firstly, he wasn't interested, so there was no point being keen. Secondly, I still had Hula Hoops on my fingers.

Ivy rolled her eyes at me and went back downstairs, saying, 'I'll tell him you're putting your make-up on.'

'Shut up!'

I plummeted downstairs after her, banging my head on a low part of the stairwell as I went. So, instead of looking nonchalant, I lurched up to the doorway rubbing my head and saying, 'Ow.'

'You OK?' said Luke. Oh. He was holding cousin Will's CD.

I nodded wordlessly.

'Here,' said Luke, handing me the CD. 'Thanks for letting me borrow it.'

'You're welcome,' I said. 'Did you – er, listen to it at all?' He couldn't have done, surely, if he was thanking me.

'Lorraine played it at my house,' said Luke. 'Earlier today, when everyone else was out.'

'Oh, OK,' I said.

Although the conversation didn't appear to be going anywhere, he didn't say goodbye or anything. It was that awkwardness again, between us, the same as when I'd watered Lorraine instead of the plants. That was it. Just like in the hall with Lorraine, he was hoping I wouldn't make things awkward by mentioning our stupid moment, the one he so clearly regretted. And coming here and just treating me like it had never happened was his way of driving the point home.

Then Luke said, 'There's something else.'

What? He wanted to come upstairs and eat Hula Hoops from my fingers? Then I realised I was still hoping. Why was I letting myself feel hurt again and again?

When I said, 'What?' it came out sounding a bit abrupt. Oops.

Luke looked at me for a moment. Then he paused and said, 'Mouse died.'

'Oh no!'

'This afternoon. Apparently he was fine when Plop went out this morning with Mum and Dad, but when she got home he was just dead in his cage. Poppy's upset so I said I'd come and tell you.'

'That's really sad.'

'Poppy's chucked out all her black stuff, so she's mourning in pink.'

Our eyes met and there was a mutual flicker of amusement. Neither of us actually said anything about it; it seemed an unsuitable moment. But then I had an awful thought.

'You played the CD . . . this morning? And Mouse died this afternoon?'

'Yes – so?' Then Luke clasped his hand to his mouth. 'Oh God – do you mean —'

'Well, we don't know for sure that it was the loud music, but . . .'

There was a troubled silence. Was it likely that an animal who couldn't even manage orange peel could have survived a prolonged dose of cousin Will's CD?

I suddenly became aware of a regular, thudding noise from inside my house.

'What's that?' asked Luke.

I turned round as Jamie came into view at the top of the stairs, in a sleeping bag completely pulled up over his head. A muffled voice emanated from the bag as he jumped down each step in turn.

'Slugman! I'm Slugman!'

He was followed by two more sleeping bags, both echoing 'Slugman!'

Luke looked from me to the sleeping bags and back again and raised his eyebrows. Mortified, I stepped outside and swiftly pulled the door almost shut. 'That's Jamie. Don't worry, he just thinks he's someone else. He never used to be like that.'

'I'm sure it can happen to the best of us,' said Luke.

I frowned at him, thinking: we don't need any more enigmatic men, thank you; Danny was quite enough.

'Well, I'd better go,' I said. 'I was just doing some, er . . . exercise.'

It was too hard, just being friends with him. Acting casual was OK, but only for short bursts.

'OK,' said Luke. 'See you.'

I nodded and went back inside. It felt sad. We had been alone, at my house, practically where we'd first kissed, but neither of us had acknowledged it. I had learned that was just the way things went. It made it seem really final, like the end. But then again, it had never really begun.

I felt a bit fragile after Mouse's funeral. We buried him on the morning of the party, under the rose bush in Poppy's back garden (sprinkling sunflower seeds on the grave as a final farewell). It was safe to say that, once I had confided my suspicions to Poppy, she no longer thought much of Lorraine. 'Mouse murderer!' she kept saying.

I went home and was quietly banging my head against the sloping bit of my bedroom wall when Ivy came in.

'What's wrong?'

I banged my head again. More slowly. So much for a brilliant Year Ten. Luke was lost, Danny turned out to be a fraud, and Mouse was dead. And autumn was coming, too. It was getting dark early and everything.

'Come on, you're not happy,' said Ivy perceptively.

'Mouse died. And Luke hates me,' I mumbled. I bumped my head again, accidentally. It hurt. I stopped.

'He doesn't hate you!' said Ivy.

OK, maybe I was being a bit melodramatic.

'Well, he just treats me as – as a friend or something.'

'I thought he fancied you!' said Ivy. I felt a momentary warmth hearing the words, but then reality kicked in.

'He doesn't. Trust me.'

'But he came round!'

'It's happened before. It meant nothing the first time either.'

And as I said the words, that was when I decided. I was moving on. It was time. I was about to have a party full of boys (well, as many boys as Sasha had managed to cobble together). This would be the perfect opportunity to snog someone new!

I summoned up the strength to move downstairs and make some tea. Jamie circled me slowly, murmuring 'Slugman!' under his breath. Just as I repressed the urge to throw teabags at him, Mum said annoyingly, 'I hope you're not going to pull a face like that tonight.'

I raised an eyebrow.

'I mean it, young lady. I'll send everyone home early.'

Quite apart from the intensely irritating 'young lady' thing, something in that sentence wasn't right.

I put down the kettle and turned towards Mum. 'You're not . . . you're not thinking of coming along, are you?'

Mum actually looked surprised! Then she said, terrifyingly, 'Of course I'm coming along. What, did you think I would let you have the run of the place by yourselves?'

Oh my God!

'We'll be fine,' I said, weak with horror.

'No way, it's dangerous,' said Mum firmly, as if a guest might be at risk of impaling themselves on a carrot stick.

'Dangerous?'

'Gangs of boys might wander in from the street – you know, in hooded tops.'

'I've got a hooded top!' I eventually managed.

'Well, yes but, you know what I mean.'

I tried not to audibly whimper.

Singin' in the Rain

Tess leaned over and popped a Toffo directly into my mouth.

'There!' she said, watching me for signs of immediate improvement. My mum had driven Poppy and me over to the badminton hall really early and made us put out games and stuff. Tess had arrived early too to help us prepare (with a string bag of lemons for the Lemon Game as well as the usual stash of confectionery) only to wander into a full-blown crisis.

I chewed the Toffo from my position of distress, horizontal on the floor of the ladies' toilets. Mercifully it was very clean in there. But, quite honestly, I was feeling a bit overwhelmed. I didn't think I could stand up. It was the thought of people from school *actually playing Jenga and badminton* rather than Spin the Bottle. I mean, Jenga! I suppose it might be exciting if you were, like, five, or had never seen bits of wood before. And . . . oh God. We'd invited boys and there was nowhere to hide them! Not even in the cloakroom, which had turned out to be just an alcove in the corridor by the entrance. It didn't even have a door!

'Calm down,' said Poppy. 'We've got a Plan A *and* a Plan B!'
I wasn't convinced.

Plan A: *Poppy and Sasha would say they invited the boys to the party and I didn't know a thing about it (Poppy and Sasha's fault).*
Plan B: *The boys would all burst in at once like a gang, wearing hooded tops (society's fault).*

I sighed and sat up. After all, I was wearing a red dress borrowed from Sasha, and I was carrying my birthday present from Tess, a little bag for my travelcard and stuff. I didn't want her to think I didn't appreciate it. And Sasha had also loaned me her highest, strappiest black heels! Tess had finished off the ensemble with hairspray and a liberal application of glitter to my neckline. I did look pretty foxy, for a change. Even if I said so myself.

'Hurrah!' said Poppy, clapping at my renewed ability to move.

'Don't worry about the Jenga. And Luke is bound to fall for you looking like that,' said Tess.

'Er . . . Tess, he won't be coming,' said Poppy.

'Oh – why not?' said Tess, crestfallen.

'What,' said Poppy, 'a party in a badminton hall? Can you see him and Lorraine doing that on a Saturday night?'

I realised with a ridiculous sinking feeling that even though I had been insisting Luke wouldn't come, I had still hoped he would be there. But Poppy was absolutely right.

'You OK?' Poppy said.

'Fine!' I replied brightly. I resolved for a second time that I would move on and Have Fun Regardless.

Tess said, 'So, we're ready! Let battle commence!'

Life did feel a bit like a battle, actually. I looked at myself in the mirror. Holly Stockwell, fifteen: physical and emotional camouflage required at all times. It was a bit depressing.

I took a deep breath and we headed into the hall.

'I knew it!' I said. 'No one's coming!'

It was just too awful. It was eight p.m. and no one had arrived! While Mum was fussing about with shuttlecocks, the three of us were just sat around playing with a bowl of Smarties, licking the red ones and applying them like lipstick.

'It will be fine,' said Poppy, as I tried not to panic. 'You said eight onwards, and it's only just eight now.'

'I thought you lot were fifteen, not five!' said a voice from behind me. We turned to see Stephen, with Sam close behind!

I gave Poppy a Look which meant, 'I didn't think he would come.' She raised her eyebrows, which meant, 'Me neither!'

I scrambled to my feet, swiftly licked the red Smartie colouring from my lips and said in a polite hostess-style voice, 'I'm glad you could both make it.'

Stephen looked me up and down and went, 'I'm very glad I came!' which was a bit random.

Out of the corner of my eye, I saw Mum abandoning the shuttlecocks and heading towards us, looking displeased, so I hurried to intercept her.

'Poppy invited some blokes from camp!' I said, trying to sound really surprised. Inspired, I added, 'Stephen, the muscular one, is a Sports Activity Leader!'

Mum looked momentarily pacified, but unfortunately Sasha chose that moment to come through the door along with her boyfriend Darren and the promised collection of male friends.

Mum sniffed and looked Unamused.

'They're here now, I suppose,' she said shortly. 'But everyone had better behave.'

GOD. I was fifteen now, in case she'd forgotten. She was such a trial. I tried not to sigh too heavily.

About an hour later things had definitely livened up. Jo and I were having a marshmallow-eating contest as I surveyed the hall full of people, delighted to have so many friends. Everyone was ignoring the badminton net and shuttlecocks, but Bethan and Rashida were challenging Darren's friends to a third round of table football in the corner. Someone had lost the ball, so they were using one of the cherry tomatoes from the buffet. Meanwhile, Poppy and Tess were watching Rachel with ill-concealed curiosity as she sat in a corner talking to Sam. I noticed in this light that Poppy's hair was beginning to wash out – back to her natural brown. She seemed really relaxed, which was good.

'Oh my God, guess who's coming in,' said Sasha, suddenly racing up to me.

'Claudia!' exclaimed my mum, racing over to the entrance. 'So nice of you to come. Did your mother drop you off?'

Marshmallows nearly fell out of my mouth, I was so surprised. Claudia walked in and looked around, acknowledging me with a thin smile.

'Why is she still annoyed?' I said to Jo, through a mouthful of marshmallow. It wasn't fair. I had tried to help! And I didn't want her hating me at my party!

'You don't understand,' said Jo, swallowing her marshmallows. 'You've seen her weakness. And now she resents you for it.'

'But how was she weak? I don't get it.'

'That's Claudia for you. It's like she's opened up to you and you now know she wants to be friends with Poppy again, but it hasn't worked. And it's something you've got! It would be easier for her if you just didn't know.'

'Blimey. It's probably just as well I didn't get Luke.'

Jo gave a horrified snort of agreement.

However, I felt a bizarre pang of understanding. It wasn't easy losing things you wanted. Maybe I could try one last time? I dashed over to Poppy, trying to ignore the look of silent outrage she was giving Claudia.

'Sorry,' I said, 'My mum invited Claudia ages ago at that sports day. I didn't think she'd actually come.'

I went quiet because Claudia was making a beeline for us! Poppy went to grab my hand, but I saw Stephen walking past and dashed after him, purposefully leaving Poppy and Claudia to sort things out.

'Having fun?' I asked Stephen hurriedly.

'Oh, yes. No Spin the Bottle tonight, though?' he said.

'Oh – you heard about that?' I said distractedly. Oh dear. I had just heard Poppy say, 'And don't try to get to me via my friends!'

Poppy walked off angrily towards Tess, and Claudia shot me an absolutely livid look. Ah – Claudia now knew I hadn't kept my vow of secrecy. But I had tried, at least.

'Shame that there's no Spin the Bottle,' Stephen repeated, looking at me intently. *Oh.* Shocked, I glanced towards Tess and Poppy, but they were clearly discussing Claudia. I had a feeling Poppy had only cut herself off from Claudia because she was still hurt. But her mind was clearly made up.

Meanwhile, Stephen had started talking about how he was a qualified instructor in something or other.

'Have you ever been paragliding, then?' he was saying, just as Poppy and Tess finally noticed us and looked gratifyingly intrigued. My phone promptly went off with a text from Tess. `Snog him!` it said.

'Oh yes, tons of times!' I found myself saying, hastily deleting the text. Para-whatting?

'Cool! When did you go?'

'Oh, I, er ... para-glid (what was the past participle?) last summer. Kept dropping the ball though.'

I felt triumphant. See. I could move on after all. It even appeared that I might get to snog someone else! Suddenly, the entrance doors swung open and Mrs Mastiff appeared.

It took Ivy to appear behind her for me to remember that I hadn't necessarily done something really bad in a former life. This was just where they trained. Mum promptly raced over to them and stood next to Mrs Mastiff, cooing over Ivy.

Poppy gave me a frantic hand signal. Aha! Now was my chance to move the team games out of sight, while Mum was distracted.

'Will you give me a hand?' I asked Stephen, who was still talking. I grabbed a bag of shuttlecocks and the game of Jenga and gave them to him to hold. On impulse I also swept up the carrot sticks from the buffet. We went through the doors to the corridor and along to the cloakroom by the entrance. I whacked everything just inside the alcove, by the coat rail.

'Can you reach those lemons?' I asked him, indicating Tess's string bag just out of reach.

Stephen leaned over to get them and as he straightened up, he went to kiss me! It was mad. 'Can you reach those lemons?' I repeated, mentally. Was that a particularly provocative line?

'I've got to go back in!' I hissed, thinking, a) It was proving surprisingly easy to snog someone else, and b) My mum was only in the hall!

'So, meet me back here in a minute,' said Stephen. He did something really weird. He kissed his fingers and briefly placed them on my lips, giving me an intense look!

Like a robot, I went back into the hall with the lemons and put them down near Tess and Poppy.

'Go for it,' said Tess, when I briefed them about the intense finger thing. 'How romantic! He's waiting for you and everything!'

'Don't be ridiculous. I can't! My mum's here! What if Mrs Mastiff needs the cloakroom or something?'

'She's still in that hideous waterproof jacket,' observed Poppy, as we all looked over. 'She's not staying.'

Tess seemed distracted by my mum's animated swiping motions with her arms. 'Is she having an epileptic fit?'

'She's praising Ivy's tennis skills,' I said without hesitating. I'd seen this millions of times before.

'Well in that case – go! While she's talking!' said Tess. 'It's really time you —'

'Got over Luke,' I finished. 'Yes. I know.'

I sighed and looked around at the hall. Tess was right. The situation reminded me of camp, when I could have snogged Danny, and hadn't. And why not? For Poppy, of course, but also for Luke – for a romance that had turned out to be a myth. I had

155

to stop being so stupid. All this was the next logical step, wasn't it? I edged sideways with one eye on Mum and Mrs Mastiff, just avoided slipping on a stray tomato from the table football, and finally slipped out towards the main entrance.

Stephen was in the cloakroom eating a carrot stick. When he saw me, he put his arms around me and pulled me just inside the cloakroom, which was all very dashing. Then he muttered, 'You look so fit!' and started snogging me!

It was half exciting and half presumptuous, and – actually, it wasn't that good a kiss. He tasted like carrots. God, you spend most of your maths lessons anticipating the next snog, and then forget how rubbish they can be.

I paused, leaned back and went quizzically, 'I didn't think you even liked me – you know, at camp?'

Stephen looked thoughtful, then said honestly, 'Well, you've done something different. I like your dress and stuff. You look, I don't know – older.'

And with that we went back into it. But, despite all my trying to move on, I remembered how I'd felt with Luke – fizzy and delirious – and how different this was. A little voice piped up in my head going, 'Why are you kissing Stephen? Isn't he just a random, carrot-eating, arrogant bloke, who only fancies you now you've got tons of make-up on?'

A song had just stopped inside and the whole scene was playing in a weird silence. I had a funny sick feeling in my stomach, and I realised I'd got it all wrong. Everyone was going around pretending, and all it seemed to do was get in the way and mess things up. I didn't have to put up a façade. I did have a choice. Suddenly I really felt like going to talk to Luke, even though nothing was going to happen between us. You know, to get rid of that splitting-in-two feeling. Otherwise he would never know what was going on in my head. And, even if he didn't care, it wasn't right to just show him a façade.

Somehow I managed to extricate myself (not easy with Stephen's tongue in my mouth), and went, 'Sorry – I need to go back in!'

I headed back into the hall and approached Poppy at speed.

'Where's my little bag?' I asked urgently. I was going to phone Luke, while I was feeling brave.

But Poppy was in a huddle with Sasha and Tess, and they all looked really agitated. What was going on?

'Did you see him?' said Poppy.

'Well, the lights were still on, so yes . . .'

'You saw Luke?'

'Luke?'

'He walked in and then out again! Just now!'

I opened and shut my mouth but no sound came out.

'He stood in the doorway for a minute,' continued Poppy, 'not looking too happy. Then he muttered something and walked out again!'

'That dark-haired girl wearing too much eyeshadow was going over to say hello to him,' added Tess breathlessly, 'but he just turned round and left again!'

Oh God, oh God. What did this mean? Luke must have seen me with Stephen. Anyone coming in late would have done. But why had he come? And what did it mean that he had come alone?

'Just act as if —' began Sasha, but I wasn't listening. I found my

157

little bag and dashed out of the hall, past the cloakroom and out into the night air. It was raining outside – that light, misty sort of rain that for some reason gets you wetter than normal rain. Drat. Where was Luke? How come he had moved so fast? I dashed to where the street joined the main road. Maybe Luke would be standing still on the rainy pavement, waiting for me to catch up with him? You know, like in a film.

However, I had forgotten again that this was South London, not America. I suddenly spotted him, further down the street! But he wasn't standing still. With exquisitely bad timing, a bus had turned up and he was getting on it!

'Oh God!' I gurgled out loud.

The thing is, I could pretend to be OK for another two months, or I could corner the bus at the next stop. The rain promptly got heavier as I took off Sasha's heels and started to run. My tights squished between my toes. God, I hated running. Although, it turned out I could go quite fast! Maybe I hadn't ever been motivated to actually *try* before?

The effort helped take my mind off how terrified I was. I'd been safe all summer, protected by my veneer of nonchalance. The possibility of allowing real feeling to surface in front of Luke was pretty scary.

Luke's bus slowed in traffic and I reached a point level with Luke's hazy outline, upstairs in his usual seat. For a moment he didn't see me, then he wiped a circle in the condensation on the window and looked down. We made eye contact as the bus abruptly lurched forwards a few metres and he was lost again.

I kept running and looked up at the sky, the rain hitting my face. Oh come on, God, I mouthed. Just this once, I want it to work out. This one's important. Although I didn't even know for sure what was going on. Or what I was going to say. Had I just messed things up by snogging Stephen?

Finally, I got on the bus, dripping with rain, only to find Luke coming down the bus stairs towards me. He looked gorgeous in his Arctic Explorer-type coat with the hood. No wonder Claudia had gone to say hello to him! We stood still for a moment, both holding on tightly, then Luke rang the bell and said, 'Let's get off.'

I saw my reflection in the bus shelter as we got off the bus. My hair was stiffly falling to one side, and my make-up had run down my face! Fortunately the shelter meant we could sit out of the rain, although it was still quite cold. I sat down gingerly on a little red plastic seat. Luke hovered for a moment, then sat down a few seats along. There was a silence.

'I didn't think you'd come,' I told him.

'Clearly!' said Luke drily. Oh God, this was going to be difficult. The thing is, I had to tell him that I still cared – that was the truth, after all. No wonder Poppy had thought it was easier to get her belly button pierced than to be herself in front of Danny.

'Am I missing something,' said Luke, 'or did we kiss at the start of the summer?'

Oh my God.

'Yes,' I said quietly, suddenly finding a discarded tin can completely fascinating. I rolled it from one foot to the other. I could feel myself unpicking the façade I'd built up painstakingly over the past month. Maybe it was weak, just like Sasha and Tess had said? But it didn't feel weak. I managed a proper sentence. 'None of my friends seemed to think the signs were that strong. You know, you only kissed me quickly on the lips, not, er – properly.'

'We were in broad daylight!'

'And I wanted to talk to you afterwards. But it felt a bit pre-sumptuous – everyone said you should make the first move. And then you acted as if nothing had happened!'

'Look,' said Luke, 'I thought it was obvious from the kiss that I wanted to go out with you but the next time I see you, you are in my house ignoring me and talking with Poppy about boys!'

'It was scary! I was going to come and talk to you, but —'

Luke interrupted me. 'So I thought, OK, you might be shy. But then I thought if you cared you might get Poppy to talk to me about it – and you didn't do that either!'

'I made Poppy promise not to embarrass me by mentioning it!'

'Oh.' Now it was Luke's turn to look down at the tin can.

'And it doesn't matter anyway,' I continued, 'because then you went off with Lorraine.'

Luke turned to look at me. 'I split up with Lorraine. Why do you think I came here by myself? That's what I was going to tell you when I came round to your house yesterday. Before, er – Slugman interrupted us.'

Oh. My. God.

'What happened?' I said, trying to restrain my joy.

'She kept saying I was really immature! She needs someone older, who's used to paying for her. And trying to get me to do all this stuff – you know, spending all my money on meals and clothes and stuff.' He sighed and then said, 'I took the clothes back to the shops today.'

I took a deep breath. Things still weren't actually resolved.

'But I told you how I felt at camp! Despite everyone telling me not to! I explained, and I told you I liked you, and you went

160

out with Lorraine anyway!'

Luke grimaced. 'Yes, you're right. But the thing is, I was with Lorraine when you called. On our first date.'

Ouch. That hurt more than my feet after all the running.

'I just thought that by then you and I would have spoken, if it was going to happen. All I'd had were negative signs. And I'd met Lorraine and she'd asked me out and she's the same age as me and . . . you know. Craig and everybody thought she was cool. Then I missed your call while I was at work and thought – well, hoped – that you'd called because you liked me. But when I called back you sounded like you were having a pretty good time without me. And I thought, well, why should I wait if you aren't interested?'

I felt doubly sick, both from Luke having been with Lorraine when I'd been speaking to him, and at the thought of Luke and Craig considering Lorraine cooler than me. Then again, I was not exactly beyond reproach, having just snogged Stephen.

'But you carried on going out with her,' I said, staring at the passing traffic, 'even though you knew I liked you.'

'I considered approaching you to sort it out – I did. Several times. But it was clear I'd messed things up. At first, when you got back, you seemed angry. And afterwards you just seemed fine. And you lent me that CD and stuff! It was pretty clear you weren't bothered at all about me and Lorraine. I figured that my behaviour had killed any feelings you'd had towards me. And, so I thought, why end it with Lorraine if I'd already blown it with you?'

I nodded dumbly, trying not to be upset. OK, so that wasn't very romantic or perfect to hear, but I guess at least he was being truthful.

'I was hurt,' I admitted. 'I'd been open with you and only got

161

humiliated. Everyone said I'd been too honest at the start and, you know, put myself on the back foot.'

'What? No, it was just really bad timing.'

'And – well . . . what was all that acting funny around me all summer? You were really awkward!'

'Yes, when I was with her!'

'You were trying to deny it had ever happened!'

'Er – no – Lorraine saw us kissing, remember? She was totally on the defensive about you and me all summer.'

'So you didn't just kiss me to make Lorraine jealous?'

Luke sat back on his red plastic seat and gave me a dumb-founded look.

'Do you really think —'

'Well, no, not now . . .' I backtracked, sensing I had gone too far.

'Look, Holly, I don't do things like that, OK? I barely even knew who Lorraine was at that point!'

I'd annoyed him now. 'Sorry,' I said meekly.

'And just now you were with Muscles, back there,' he added, sounding wounded.

'He's just someone from camp. It was stupid. A spur-of-the-moment-type thing.' I continued, 'Why didn't you tell me you'd split up with Lorraine when you came to my house?'

'You were acting all casual again. I got scared.'

'But you're telling me now?'

'Only because you ran after me. Before that, I didn't know if – I wondered, after I touched your hand on the bus, if you still cared. It seemed as if I'd caught you off guard. So I came round. But I wasn't sure. It was too scary to ask you.'

Luke kicked away the tin can with his foot, then leaned over and put his arm around me. I realised I was shivering from the cold.

'You are stronger than me,' he said.

I don't think I am very good with compliments, because all I could say was, 'You should be singing.'

'What?'

'*I can see clearly now Lorraine has gone . . .*' I sang. Then I spoiled it by laughing at my own rubbish joke.

He looked as if he was going to dig me in the ribs. But he didn't. Instead he pulled me towards him and kissed me! This time, it was full on the lips. With tongues. I kissed back, tangled up in the sensation, smelling his aftershave, feeling the warmth of his body around me. I hadn't been sure if the first kiss had meant anything. But I knew this one definitely did.

Once Upon a Time in South London

Monday at school was legendary. Yes, even with Mme Tournon circling the French lesson on her endless pronunciation mission. She was teaching us to roll our *r*'s, but unsurprisingly our efforts wouldn't do.

'Rer-rer-rer,' we all repeated, hopelessly.

'Practise in groups,' she sighed and started pacing the room.

Excellent. Poppy, Sasha, Jo and I all huddled in to talk properly.

'Holly, you've still got glitter on you,' observed Jo in low tones.

'You should see Luke!' said Poppy.

'Shut up!' I said, delightedly.

'So what happened?' whispered Jo. 'I can't believe I had to leave early.'

'It was so lovely,' I whispered back. 'After we kissed at the bus stop, he gave me his coat because I was cold and wet. It was too big on me. It was lovely and warm and smelled of Lynx.'

I risked a cautious glance towards Claudia, who was on the other side of the aisle in a group with Bethan, Charlotte and Rashida. I was in no hurry to tell her my news.

Claudia looked up and said bluntly, 'I can hear you, you know.'

Oh.

'I bet you're delighted now, aren't you?' she said, her voice coming out all squeaky.

I sat speechless, thinking, 'God, mad woman alert.' I realised her hatred of me had just increased ten-fold. In her eyes, I had Poppy, and I had Luke, and I was Public Enemy Number One. It didn't seem fair, really. I didn't feel like I'd done anything wrong!

Sasha raised her eyebrows at Claudia.

'Then what happened?' said Jo, speaking more quietly.

'Er, that's when I went back to the party. I had to go back. Luke went home, so my mum wouldn't be suspicious.'

'I texted Holly,' Poppy told Jo, 'because her mum kept asking "Where's the Jenga? And where's Holly?"'

In order of importance, I thought.

'I meant to ask,' I said, 'while I was gone, did you get to play the Lemon Game?'

'No,' said Poppy gloomily. 'You put them down on the buffet table. By the time I noticed, your mum had sliced them up and put them in the Coca Cola! Tess scrunched up bits of wrapping paper instead, but it didn't work very well.'

'It worked for some people,' said Sasha.

'What do you mean?'

'While you were gone I saw your friend – the quiet one – snog that bloke Sam!'

Oh my God! 'Rachel?'

'Yes! One minute she had to pass the wrapping paper to him and the next they were snogging!'

'Not in the hall?'

'I made them go into the cloakroom,' Poppy reassured me. 'Oh, and Rachel gave me a flip-flop she thinks is yours. She knew it wasn't hers because it didn't have a name tag on it.'

'Ooo!' interrupted Mme Tournon, suddenly giving up on rolling *r*'s. '*Dessous. Oo. Répétez.*'

'Ooo,' we chorused obediently.

'*Non!*' Mme Tournon sighed heavily. 'Practise.'

I turned back towards our little group. 'It's not all perfect. Apparently I'm still on the cross-country team.'

Poppy giggled far too much, considering it was not AT ALL funny. 'Mrs Mastiff left in her car and drove along the main road —'

'And saw me running after Luke's bus.' I finished gloomily. 'Apparently I was going pretty fast.'

'So – with Luke – is it really happening this time?' said Jo.

'We're definitely going out together!'

Jo's eyes widened. 'Ooh!'

With that, Mme Tournon stopped circling the room and beamed with pride. '*Oui,* Jo! *Très bien!*'

So we thought we had better stop talking and actually do some work, for this French lesson at least. But it was fine. I knew that, from this point on, I would have lots of interesting thoughts to keep me awake.

THE END

166

Find out how it all started!

In the back of my rough book I wrote a list of hurdles I
needed to overcome in order to meet Luke and some of his
friends in town for an almost-date type situation.

1. *Get Poppy to invite Jez.*
2. *Phone Luke (ignoring obvious further hurdle of family*
   listening in while I talk on landline).
3. *Possibly clarify to Luke who I am.*
4. *Present compelling reasons as to why Luke would want*
   to agree to the above, along with his friends, whom I've
   never met.

Meet Holly Stockwell, fourteen. She hates all forms of
exercise, gets tongue-tied around boys, and her best
friend, Poppy, seems to be developing a *new* best friend
– the rich and gorgeous Claudia! Can she overcome
these traumas without life getting any worse?

ISBN: 978 1 85340 851 9

www.piccadillypress.co.uk

☆ The latest news on forthcoming books

☆ Chapter previews

☆ Author biographies

☆ Fun quizzes

☆ Reader reviews

☆ Competitions and fab prizes

☆ Book features and cool downloads

☆ And much, much more . . .

Log on and check it out!

Piccadilly Press